I0710714

The

Jade

Commander

F.L. Journey

Paperback ISBN-13: 978-1-965176-08-5

Ebook ISBN: 978-1-965176-07-8

For information please contact publisher at faireydragonpress@gmail.com

Table of Contents

Dedication

To our readers for joining up on this journey. Thank you for the support.

1

During the Titan War

She could hear the footsteps closing in behind her, but she had to keep moving. Running up a small embankment, she slid down the other side. As she stopped, she saw a tree with a hole at eye level. She could hear his voice, but nothing would stop her now. She tore off the pouch which one day could save them. The pouch had been on her neck for the last week. Knowing her death was imminent, she had to keep the stone safe from him. Sliding the pouch into the hole, she stood back and looked at the hiding spot. The little pouch was completely hidden. Confident the stone would not be easily found, she took off again.

Minutes later, the hunters came over the embankment. One paused momentarily by the tree before catching her movement deeper in the forest.

"Hurry hunters, the commander will give us hell if the Titan escapes." The higher ranked hunter breathed heavily.

Barely slowing, they continued after the running woman.

"She's close, I can smell the filth."

Themis burst through a small thicket of trees into a massive clearing.

No, she thought. She knew this would be her last stand, but at least there was still hope, she was thinking about the small package in the tree. She looked down at the slight bump hidden by her clothes, I am sorry child. She drew a short sword which had been concealed by her cloak and readied herself.

Unbeknownst to them, an orb of light had unceremoniously been following at a distance. The orb had flitted here and there as it continued through the forest with a purpose still unknown to it. Upon reaching the tree, the orb moved closer and closer until it was all but touching the large oak tree. It floated motionlessly, waiting. Slowly, the wisp moved into the tree.

In the distance, a woman could be heard screaming. But nothing mattered to the little wisp. It had found its purpose, its new life.

The clang of swords echoed through the forest as the tree began to twist and writhe; its leaves fell to the earth, and branches began to change until only two limbs remained as arms. The smaller branches began to twist in the wind like strands of silky hair. The roots ripped themselves out of the ground, forming into legs.

As one young woman was seeing her life slip away another was just beginning.

The tree now lay still. The howling wind no longer rustled its leaves. The once great oak now lay naked on the ground, transformed into a beautiful woman with greenish skin, the color of olives and a red heart made of stone. Stretching in the sunlight, the woman looked around and continued her journey. Ignoring the sounds deeper in the woods.

In the clearing, one hunter lay motionless in the tall grass, blood soaking the earth.

"You will never have me," Themis said, swinging her blade toward the remaining would-be capturers.

"You sure are a feisty little Titan. It's too bad you chose the losing side," spoke the man dodging the blade.

"We shall see, won't we?" Her blade followed her words, and another man hit the ground gasping for breath he would never find.

As soon as he fell still, another emerged from the tree line. "End this now, just come along. The war is over and has been for a while. Your side lost," the tall man holding a staff spoke.

Fear tore through her. It was him, the commander of the legions of gods. The bringer of death.

"Sir, she is mine." The last hunter stepped toward the frozen woman only to fall still as the blade of a chakram embedded in his neck.

"Disobedience is unacceptable, hunter." Loathing and disgust escaped with his words as he retrieved the blade from the dead man's body. "Now Themis, it's time to join the others. Think of your child. Its father is already dead; don't leave it an orphan."

"Why are you doing this?" The woman fell to her knees as the man approached. "Please don't do this, Jannes."

Off in another part of the forest walked a newly free woman. She walked, amazed by the trees and the light refracting through the leaves and branches. She continued until a small house near a beautiful fountain came into view. Kneeling near the fountain, with its hands full of stones, was a small creature who resembled a manly frog. He was running the stones between his fingers and chatting with himself.

"Hello, I seem to be lost. Who are you?" the woman said, approaching the man.

He turned and the woman took his breath away. The stones all clattered to the ground, suddenly unimportant. "My, aren't you pretty? My name is Menninkainen, what is yours?" Looking around before continuing. "As for where you are, this is my forest." He stood, spreading his arms wide. "You are more than welcome to stay a while if you wish. These times are dangerous with some Titans still roaming the world, especially for a young woman as pretty as you." The small goblin offered his hand to her.

"My name is Meredith. Thank you for your hospitality. I think I will stay a bit." She took his hand.

Cee walked up to Jan and shook him gently. "Jan, get out of your head, and tell us what you know!"

"I called Erato, and she was trying to piece together what happened. Apparently, a group of Dryads went to an event in the wilderness. Some tree thing they do biannually. Meredith was with them. Erato is pregnant with a set of twins so she couldn't go. She got a call at around midnight from one of the Dryads screaming. Erato tried to get more info, but the line went dead."

"What were they screaming? It takes a lot to affect a Dryad." Theo remembered the Dryads during the wars.

"She was screaming 'hyena' over and over. It didn't mean anything to Erato. There are no hyenas in the forest. She said she sent a response team, but she didn't know how long it would take for them to get there." Jan finished with his head in his hands.

The four looked at each other. Cee took a deep breath. "The shadow leader, the one who attacked us, who killed Brandy's father? The one Brandy's older brother Oran was working for. His brand is a hyena, isn't it? A hyena with a mane of snakes.

"Why would they go after Dryads? It just doesn't make any sense," Jan said. "They keep to themselves."

"I don't know, Jan. I really don't know, and we can't be sure it's even the same group. Could someone be starting the war over? It's a pretty big coincidence, but they could be making their move. Whatever it is, we'll figure it out as a family."

"Jan, I'll go with you. We don't know what we'll find. Cee can stay home and manage the gate. But we do need to tell Hades. Whatever has been moving in the shadows, I think it's about to show its face." Theo put his hand on his brother's shoulder.

"I'll call him, just give me a couple minutes." Panterra reached out to Theo, and he handed her his phone. She disappeared into another room, and after mere moments she returned. Panterra walked back into the dining room. "He wants us all at the Vineyard, now."

"I'm going as well. The Gate can stay closed for the time being because this is more important." Cee grabbed Brandy's hand. "We are family and will face this as family."

Jan sat in the backseat of Theo's Land Rover with two dogs and a cat. He thought about the first time he had met Meredith. Until then he hadn't known much about Dryads other than in passing.

***

Cee looked up from the gate and noticed a reaper in tattered clothes.

"I need Jan, where is he?" the newcomer asked.

Jan appeared from behind Cee. "What do you want?"

"Sir, we need you. So many of us have died, and the souls are in chaos. The war has been won but we just can't manage."

Jan shook his head. "Why so much death, what was the need?" he asked no one. Years ago, he had lusted for the battlefield. A game of chess, pawns being sent to their death without a second thought. But it no longer sat right with him. His own soul did not sit right. It felt like it was trying to escape the horrors of his past.

"Jan, it's okay. I can go in your stead."

"No, I started this, so I should be the one who goes." He walked up to the Reaper. Within a moment, the scent of death filled his nostrils.

"This doesn't seem right. What did these people do to deserve this?" Jan asked the Reaper as they walked across a trampled grain field. Helpless souls, confused from the suddenness of death, floated around aimlessly.

"Commander Jan, you led the great God army against the Titans centuries ago. It is you whom I have come to admire, and many of my tactics were yours." Looking around, the Reaper stepped closer. "This war was not fair, and it's hard for me to bear witness as my own are there among the dead. But they should not be. I had heard stories of the Titan Wars, and I remember when you said, 'for the greater glory of all we will conquer those who oppose'. I have lived by those words. But where were you for this war?"

Screams filled Jan's ears. Screams of those long gone. Screams which have plagued him for centuries. He could still feel the blood on his hands, the warmth on his skin chilling him to the bone. Slowly, he wiped his hands on his pants hoping it would wipe the memories away as well. He didn't care if the Reaper noticed.

Jan thought about his part in the great war but had never dwelled on it more than he did now. The bodies of many different creatures spread out before him. The moans from the forest, real or perceived, cast a shadow over his mind. Since the war ended, he had been one of the guardians of the gate with his two brothers. But Jan understood the toll war had on his own soul all too well. He was called to command units during this war, but he had refused. He couldn't sleep as it was, and the blood in his dreams flowed too swiftly. For days on end, he used his family as a crutch to stand in front of the great gate. He was never far from his brothers.

Sure, Theo fought, but he didn't have to. He chose to, but he never left for long. Just long enough to save some damsel or thwart a coup. He was Hades' sword after all, the infamous 'Warrior Dog'. Jan scoffed. Theo had created the name for himself during the Titan War.

Jan was a leader, born and raised as the oldest to lead not only their family unit, but what turned out to be vast militaries when needed.

It was no different than Cee being a listener and thinker, or Theo a fighter. They all grew up with their parts to play. His experience with war was different, but as real as a Reaper's. He wasn't in the trenches or in the fields. He was in a room, looking at maps and deciding where to send people, where to send what amounted to ants, to oblivion.

Jan had spent his fair share of time on the fronts, but his true skill was as the overlord. Now in this war, he only saw the aftermath. He saw the coins as they arrived, and many did not even really understand what the coins were.

War happened, and both the Reapers and the brothers understood it was a part of life and the growth of civilization. But these Dryad wars were something completely different. This was not a war; this was annihilation. Jan had realized early on this was the killing of innocents. Yes, there were those who actively fought against the Reaper units, but for the most part, they were killing those without weapons. Why the wardens would have started such a campaign, he didn't know.

As Jan and the Reaper walked the battlefield, they came to a group of trees. This would not have normally given Jan pause, but something felt out of place. Jan looked around as the Reaper general continued praising the old wars and comparing his likeness to the solders of the past.

The battle had flattened the countryside, so nothing stood but these trees. Jan continued to ignore the Reaper and walked among the trees. He noticed they didn't move like normal trees.

The wind ruffled his hair, but the leaves were silent. The Reaper continued his diatribe as he walked to the next group of souls.

Jan, however, felt drawn to the trees and stopped near one with an elegant and soft green color. As he did, what he had originally believed to be knots opened into beautiful green eyes. They ripped into his soul and soothed him, the warmth of his chilled hands calming.

He knew what these trees were now. Jan glanced at the Reaper still talking to himself and wondered how these Dryads had survived the war. How lucky they were this general was a fool. He walked closer and put his hand on the tree. The eyes grew fearful and closed. "Don't fear me. I will not hurt you."

The eyes opened back up and looked at him cautiously. Jan held up both hands showing he did not possess a weapon.

Slowly, the tree began to transform into a slender woman. She was more than a head shorter than Jan. Her height caused him to look over top her green hair. She looked up at him, trembling.

"Is the battle over? Are you going to hurt us?"

"Us? Are there more of you? The battle is over, the war is over. I'm here to gather the wandering souls, not make more. I won't hurt you or whoever else there is. I am a guardian, not a killer."

That was mostly true, but if forced, Jan could wield his deadly chakrams. He had vowed not to again, but he could, and would, if the cause was true.

She nodded and walked around the rest of the trees. "Sisters, it is over. We are safe." She eyed Jan carefully, putting a smile on the tainted man.

All at once the rest of the trees began to transform into women, young and old. The only thing they had in common was their hair and skin were shades of green. In total, there were twenty Dryads now all standing around Jan and looking at him for answers.

The woman he had first met walked up to him. "My name is Meredith, and we are in need of food and a place to rest."

Jan looked down into her eyes again and felt them pierce his soul, seeming to be studying it, trying to understand. Jan looked up realizing the Reaper general was no longer talking. His eyes roamed the beautiful green locks and fell on the man he had so recently partnered with. The Reaper was standing, still sword in hand, with a look of hatred on his face.

"No, these are not soldiers. The war is over!" Jan yelled on deaf ears as the man advanced.

Meredith whispered, "It's the inquisitor." She looked at Jan, drawing his gaze. "Please help us."

Another in the group also recognized the Reaper. "It's the Inquisitor! Gods help us." Panic had thrown the group into chaos, and most of the Dryads had fallen to the ground weeping. The only one who stepped forward was Meredith.

Tears fell down her cheeks and dampened her green skin. Her bare feet fell silently on the dirt as she moved toward the slayer of her people.

"I will not go quietly."

She lifted a hand, partially transformed, into a sharp branch and held it like a sword. But her view became obscured by another. By the man who she felt drawn to.

"No, it ends here. I will allow no more unnecessary death, Reaper," Jan growled.

The approaching man paused in thought. "You know how many of my kind they killed? How many I watched die? I vowed long ago this world will be rid of Dryads if it is the last thing I do."

Jan looked him over, studying the twisted man. "Then it will be the last thing you do."

"Stand aside. You have no allegiance to them, so walk away while you still can. Or are you a sympathizer?" The Reaper liked his last words, as they swelled him with pride. "I will kill the Great Cerberus Commander and take his head to my liege, the Shadow Lord." He rushed Jan.

Before the Reaper had closed on him, Jan summoned his chakrams. The Reaper was so consumed with rage and pride he fell easily to the eldest brother. Jan kicked the Reaper in the chest as he came close enough, sending him to the ground. The downward blow from his circular blade ended the attacker swiftly and quietly.

Jan looked down at the blood dripping from his weapons. He could feel the chill returning just as his body was trying to reject it. And just as it started, it was gone. Jan looked down to see a thin, green hand on his arm. He followed the hand to the body and eyes of the young Dryad who in part just saved his life.

Meredith looked at him in earnest before turning to the rest of the group. "It is okay. I trust the tall man." Right then, a union was created.

"That rat, I can't believe the gall of him. After everything I did for him." As the group entered the boardroom, Hades was storming around the room. Smoke was literally coming from the top of his head. On the floor near Hades were broken bottles of wine, pinot noir to be precise. From the lack of liquid amongst the glass, it looked like the bottles had been empty, which means Hades was at least 4 bottles deep. Sammy and Diego immediately moved behind the legs of Jan and Theo, respectfully. Cleo on the other hand, strode up to the table, jumped up, and walked toward Hades. Leave it to a cat to ignore the sure signs of pure danger, thought Cee.

Panterra whispered to Cee, "Is Persephone here?"

Cee whispered back, "No, she's still with her family for another couple of weeks. We cannot call her because her family lives on a commune or something. They don't allow phones. Her family are all about the silence, self-power, and nature, or something."

"There's nothing wrong with that. Sometimes I think we need more nature in our lives." Panterra thought about her druid friend.

"Will you two shut it?" Jan looked back at them before turning to Hades.

"Hades, I don't have time for your tantrums. Stop pacing and speak your mind," Jan snapped.

"I don't know what he's up to, but I know who it is," Hades said, making eye contact with Jan now.

"Who?!" Jan yelled, finally at his wit's end.

"The shadow behind all of it. I know it's Set. It must be him. Especially with the brand from the armor and then the coin. It took me a while to figure out, but it's his brand from ancient times. From the Titan War, actually. I had been looking at the gods but not the Titans."

A large book materialized on the table in front of Hades. Looking around, Hades gestured to the others to sit. Sammy and Diego looked between the brothers and Hades and curled up at the foot of the table. Close enough to be there if something went wrong but far enough to not be singed if Hades decided to trade the smoke for fire.

"This book was created at the end of the Titan Wars. Think of it has an address book for gods." As it slid across the table, Cleo attempted to bat at it, but it was moving too fast. When it was out of her reach, she laid back down near Hades who absently started petting her.

Jan opened the book to the front page where a list of names appeared.

"They aren't in order. Or at least any order I can determine." Jan looked toward Hades as Cee looked over the page.

"That's because they're from weakest to strongest. When a God dies, they stay in the book, but if you flip to the second page, you'll see Sopek's name crossed out." As Jan flipped through the pages, he saw some names he recognized, and a few had a strike through their name.

Before he could get much further in the book, Hades motioned for it back. The book closed and slid back to him. As it sat on the table, Cleo was able to play with the book.

Brandy hissed, but Cleo paid no attention to her.

"So, each entry for the God has their information. What part or element they control, where they reside, what they like to eat, and who they follow. However, no matter how long you look, there is nothing in this book about Set."

The brothers looked at each other confused.

"Then why the theatrics? Why show us the book?" Theo asked, finally speaking.

"It's because Set is in this other book." Another book flew from an oak bookcase and landed in front of Jan. On the front cover was a word in an ancient language, but one Jan knew all too well. The single word translated to 'The Titans'.

"Wait, how is there a Titan free on the land?" Jan spoke up, remembering the end of the war. "They were all imprisoned in the furnace. I was there when the last was forced through the gate."

"I didn't know. He said he had fought in the southern wastelands," Hades said, disgusted at his revelation.

"Don't you think it was careless not to know, after all the death, all the loss?!" Jan yelled, pounding his fists on the table.

Hade's resolve faded. He grew to his full height and looked down on the unyielding Jan.

Jan's outburst was surprising considering Hades was the King of the Underworld and more powerful than all three brothers combined.

"You do not get to question me; you only get to listen!" The temperature in the room jumped as Hades yelled.

The two did not back down, and what seemed like eons passed before Theo put his hand on his brother's shoulder, breaking the tension.

"Anyways, after Sopek died, his name was crossed out, but on his page..." Hades sat and flipped to the page with a small bookmark sticking out of the top with a small feather attached to the edge. No one had initially noticed the bookmark, but now Cee understood why Cleo had wanted to paw at it. "...there is no information about who killed him or why. I wasn't really worried about it because his Reapers pledged fealty to Panterra, and everything seemed to balance out again." Hades again flipped through pages.

"However, in the last two days we have seen a couple of other lesser and mid-level gods die without reason or the killer's name. Those events began to worry me. All gods are connected, and it's impossible to hide nefarious acts from the book."

Cee practically licked his lips staring in awe at the book.

In a sudden movement, Hades got up and walked to the wine closet behind him. Taking out another bottle of wine, he turned around, lifting it while uncorking it.

All three brothers and two ladies shook their heads.

He shrugged and poured himself a glass. Returning to his seat, he leaned back. "So maybe I should back up. This book was created right after the Titan Wars." Sensing Cee's interest, Hades poured another glass of wine before he started his tale.

"During the Titan Wars when we knew we were going to win, the Gods decided two things. First, we decided the Titan's fate, and then we had to decide how to handle all the lost souls. Banishing the Titans to the Furnace was an easy decision, but the creation of the Underworld you see now was far more difficult. We went through multiple meetings and ideas until someone presented a plan for a unified Underworld, one where the lost souls could find themselves and be at peace. However, with the Gods winning the war and the Titan's ideology being suppressed, it was determined all souls should be sequestered somewhere in a single place until the world was calmed. This was the opposite of the souls having free movement among the planes of the living as was desired by the Titans. Which, as we knew, started the War."

"Wait, so the Underworld hasn't always existed?" Panterra asked. "Did Reapers not always exist?" Pantera was shaken to her core.

Hades looked down into his wine glass and his memories. "Yes and no, I will get to that, if it's okay with you."

"Of course," she said begrudgingly. Even though Panterra was strong, she wasn't stupid. She was still in the presence of Hades, the Lord of the Underworld.

"Remember Panterra, I wasn't always the leader of the Underworld. I was just a God without a home who led soldiers. I was in love once. I was young and inexperienced," Hades said with sadness in his eyes.

"So how did you become the leader?" Brandy asked out of nowhere, hearing it all for the first time.

"That's where the story continues." Hades sipped his Vino.

"After a meeting between the leaders of the dead, it was determined a committee would be formed. We called ourselves, unofficially, the house of the Templar. Those from each region would send a representative and meet in Greece. At the time, it was the center of the world. After infighting and disagreements, our committee was formed, and I was chosen as leader. I was forced to designate Set as my second. He had ran to his boss and demanded a position. It was above my control and so I had to do it. Hecate became my left hand while Set was my right. Mania, who had originally fought for control, took over as the Goddess of the death bringers. Other culture's Gods maintained their positions. They each maintained a small contingent of Reapers, and essentially everything trickled down from there." Hades paused, waiting for a response.

"So that's how Mania became leader of the Reapers?" Panterra asked. She had met Mania once but didn't know she was 'the' leader of the Reapers.

"Essentially, yes. It was much more convoluted, and other cultures were upset about it. But ultimately, she was the queen of the Reapers. While technically she still is, she has given up a lot of her responsibilities to explore other passions. As you know, the leadership structure especially lately."

"So, then what happened?" Brandy was on the edge of her seat. Some of the information was already known to the brothers, and to a lesser extent Panterra, but with Brandy being new, she was still in awe of everything.

"Not much, we created the great stone gate alongside the fire gates of the furnace. One could not be without the other. The coins were needed, they were…" Hades paused, "with Set being number two, we tried to control it all, but we knew we could not guard the gates and rule the underworld. Soon, we both realized we couldn't do it alone, and that's where the Cerberus come in. You took over control of the Gates with the wardens and oversaw the flow of Reapers and the souls."

"Jeez, thanks Hades," Theo quipped.

"You don't have to do it every day like I had to. Set would go missing for weeks, or in some cases, years.

I never knew why. I never knew his true nature." Hades put his wine down, having now settled his nerves.

"But why do you think everything goes back to Set?" Cee asked, eyeing the second book, wanting to get his hands on it.

"Set was really unhappy when I took over. He had been vetted by an Egyptian god. I thought things had gotten better, but during the Dryad wars when I brought the brothers on as my stand-ins, he literally threw a tantrum. Hundreds died. Now I know he was a wolf in sheep's clothing, I understand why. He wanted to open the furnace. He wanted to destroy everything we had built. What we sacrificed so much to obtain." He looked deep into his wine glass sitting on the table. This time, they all noticed.

Brandy wanted to know more. "Why are you so sad when you talk about the gates?"

Cee jabbed her in the ribs.

She turned to him. "What? I know you noticed it too."

..Hades ignored the outburst and continued his tale. "I sent Mania after Set to understand why he was becoming so intolerable. She came back different."

"I had forgotten, but I think I was there," Jan spoke up.

***

Hades had just finished briefing Jan when Mania stumbled into his office. Rushing to help her, he sat her in the chair opposite Jan.

"Mania, are you okay? What happened?" Hades implored after Jan brought her something to drink, before both men sat back down.

"It was bad. It wasn't what we thought it was going to be. Set—It was supposed to be Set's prison."

"Wait, what do you mean?"

"The fire, the endless fire, does not lick at his boots. He is free, he is free." Her eyes went black as she recalled a memory.

"It is horrible Hades. The souls. The pain the pain." She tore at her hair, eyes closed, shaking in the chair.

"Mania, you were gone for months. What happened?" Hades was worried.

"Months? No, years. Years of misery. I was only gone forever. All my life..." she said, looking straight through Jan like he wasn't there.

"Mania, it has been..." Hades checked the tablet in front of him. Counting the hash marks he had made, he looked back at her. "What happened to you?"

The remaining light in Mania's eyes started to dim. Shaking her head, she stood unsteadily. She began to look around frantically, her eyes clearing for a minute.

"What of Manus? Is he still alive? Where is he?" Jan spoke, remembering his second in command had traveled with her.

"Why are you so shaken? What has happened?" Hades was concerned by how Mania was acting. She had been named the Titan Reaper during the war. She had been through the worst without any noticeable issues. What could cause her this much distress?

"I have a home. Yes, I have a home," she said, her eyes rolling back as if trying to see something.

"Mania, do you know if Manus lives?" Jan again tried to break into her mind.

She only looked at him.

Jan stood and rested his hand on Mania's elbow. "Come, let's get you to your family. It isn't far."

Upon returning to Hades' office, Jan knocked quietly on the door. It slowly opened on its own, and Jan saw Hades with a large book on his desk. One hand flipped through the pages, and the other worrying his hair.

"Hades, you requested my return?" Jan said.

"Yes Jan, thank you. Did Mania get home safely? I am greatly concerned about what is happening in the Underworld. I feel I'm losing control."

"Do you wish for me to go see what's happening?"

"No! At least not until we are able to learn what happened from Mania. I can't risk you," Hades responded while slamming the book closed.

4

"It was the last time I mentioned going to the Underworld, and the last time Hades had mentioned Set or any other issues. I figured it went away," Jan said calming down.

Hades sat forward in his chair. "As did I. I sought some additional support for you at the gate. I also called Set into my office and spoke to him. While he denied keeping Mania captive for those years, he did admit to using the souls for his own purposes. He stated he would stop, and when I sent another in centuries later, he had. There was no reason for me to believe he would do it again or he would do something else so underhanded. But it seems he has, which leads me to—" He paused for a second.

Hades smiled. "Ah Cybele. Yes, we were having a dinner one evening with Gods and Goddesses I knew were loyal, and I told them about my fears. They all agreed we needed to keep the Cerberus safe, and Cybele had the idea."

Brandy looked at Cee and smiled. She knew Cee and Cybele had a relationship in the past. Initially, it was weird for her to be dating, actually engaged, to the same individual her mother had dated. But her love for Cee had eventually won over her conflict of being with someone her mother had been in a relationship with. Not that she had known who, or what, her mother was until recently.

"As you know, she had the stones made to give powers to animal companions. Usually dogs." Hades looked at Cleo, who was doing her best impression of a bread loaf while napping. "But sometimes cats."

Everyone chuckled as it had only been Cee who'd had a cat companion, and Cleo was only his second cat in centuries.

"When Set found out about the companions, he demanded to know everything there was to know about them. I told him some, but obviously not everything. So, I was as surprised as you were when the bounty was placed on Turk's head. Again, I'm sorry for your loss, Cee."

Brandy reached out and held Cee's hand. The death of Turk had taken a lot out of him, and they were all still worried about him. Cleo had been a good distraction, especially since she was a lot like Turk. Just with longer fur and more napping.

"Obviously, I had to tell him something because I had told Hecate a lot, being she was my left hand. With Set being my right, I still had hope he wasn't intentionally trying to do anything against the Gates or the Underworld."

"Since the Gates moved to Hood River a little more than 300 years ago, Set hadn't done anything that would cause me to rethink my earlier assessment regarding him changing. However, recent events make me think he had, in fact, traveled further down his original road. The brand we keep seeing is one such thing." Hades poured himself another glass of wine.

"When Set had first came to the meeting and was given the position of Hades' second in command, his symbol had been a red-haired beast with a forked tongue. Being he was the God of chaos, it was no surprise his symbol would be an animal that caused fear. Over time, his symbol changed to a griffin, then a crocodile. He never stayed with any one thing. The last time I saw him he was talking about how many in the Underworld felt him to be a hyena because of how he had treated people."

"So, the Hyena is explained, but what about the snakes?"

"I remember a story being told about Set, Ra, and snakes," Hades commented as he leaned back in his chair to think.

"Before given the position in the Underworld when Set was still in Egypt, the Sky God Ra ran into an issue. One day Ra was stopped while travelling across the sky by Apophis, who was a serpent. Apophis was able to freeze Ra in place using their gaze. However, Set was nearby and able to resist the gaze and therefore able to save Ra. Set's power grew among his people, but he wanted more, always wanted more. So, when the position came up, he wanted it. As we all know, this is just the story behind the truth. This truth was always unknown to me. I have been asking about this tale recently. I found someone who was there when Apophis fought Ra in the Titan War." Hades paused again, taking a long sip. "I should have pressed earlier but Set knew the war was coming to an end, and he was apparently Apophis's second not only during the war, but also for succession of Apophis' position."

Theo gasped at the thought.

"You mean to tell me your second in command of the entire underworld, and the one overseeing the Furnace was the right hand of Apophis, the ruthless and brutal leader of the Titans? The one who almost single handedly wiped out two garrisons before Ra's struck him down?!"

Theo's eyes were wide as he moved his head back and forth between a raging Cee and Hades, waiting for a response.

Hades' shoulders sank. "Yes, from what I know now Set helped Ra kill Apophis, and in return for his betrayal, Ra agreed to hide his true nature and push for his involvement in the gates."

"But what does that have to do with the symbol?" Brandy chimed in.

"It was his battle flag during the war." Hades ended with, downing his glass before pouring another.

"I guess that explains the Hyena and the Snakes. And why is he now going after you? Why is he showing his hand?" Jan asked.

Hades flipped to a specific page in the book before sliding it to the middle of the table again. On the page was Set's name, followed by a list of information about him. Next to the information was a brand similar to the one Brandy, Cee, Panterra, and Theo had encountered in Ireland.

The group crowded around the book trying to glean as much information as possible about Set and why he could be doing it.

"This doesn't say why he's doing what he's doing." Cee flopped back in his chair with a look of dismay.

"He helped create the book, so he only allows what he wants to be included. This brand just showed up this morning, even though we all know he's been using it for much longer. So, it's safe to assume he's hiding other things."

"What's the plan though, like what do we know or not know? Is Meredith part of this plan?" Jan asked, already trying to formulate an attack.

"I don't know. I wish I did. I have questions out to allies, and we will figure it out. The best course of action is to live life normally and wait for his next move."

"I can't wait for his next move if it involves Meredith!" Jan stood facing Hades. Sammy stood with her teeth bared.

Both Theo and Cee stood and moved toward Jan. Both in support of him seeking answers and to calm him down.

"Do you really think I would let something happen to her?" Smoke puffed off the top of Hades' head again.

Panterra reached over and grabbed Brandy's hand. Let's go, she mouthed as she pulled Brandy toward the door. Once they got outside and the door clicked behind them, Panterra turned toward Brandy.

"It'll be okay. They get into arguments like this sometimes. Hades cares a great deal for the Cerberus brothers, and by extension Meredith, me, and you now you're with Cee. He won't hurt them..." Panterra looked back toward the door as smoke started seeping under. "...on purpose. They have a volatile relationship sometimes."

"But why? I mean aren't the brothers just working for Hades? Why does he care about all of us so much?" Brandy squeaked out as the door shook.

"I honestly don't know. When I met Theo, they had already been working for Hades for centuries. I know they were with him during the Dryad war. I think they're more like family at this point than just workers. I've never asked Theo, and I don't even know if he knows. Cee may know because he's more of the historian and scholar of the group. Theo just likes to break things." Panterra chuckled as she led Brandy into the vineyard's tasting room.

Diana, who was a good friend of Theo's, was behind the counter.

"Afternoon ladies. Can I get you a drink?" Initially, Diana and Panterra had gotten off on the wrong foot. Diana had liked Theo, but Theo didn't want to be with her for a variety of reasons. Then Panterra showed back up, and Diana realized she and Theo were better off as friends. Panterra actually helped Diana get a job at Hades' vineyard as the tasting room manager. "Panterra, I keep forgetting to thank you for getting me this interview. I love this job."

"No problem, what are friends for?" Panterra smiled before looking at the list of wines currently available. "Brandy, do you want anything? The reds are really quite good."

Brandy, still taken back by Panterra's nonchalance at leaving the brothers to Hades, shook her head a bit before deciding on a blush. "I will take a glass of ambrosia."

"And I'll take a glass of 6 of red."

As Diana went to get their wine, Brandy looked on. "Does she know? Is she... you know, like us?"

"No, she's human as far as everyone knows. She does know some about us. Well, she didn't originally, but she's dating Basil. So, she got a crash course in all this."

"Is that bad? I mean, couldn't she tell our secrets or something?" Brandy kept looking back toward the office.

"Yes, I guess she could, but who would believe her? She doesn't know everything. She knows enough to keep her safe at work, but not enough to make her unsafe."

"What do you mean?" Brandy asked, confused.

Diana walked back with their glasses along with a glass of white wine. "She means if someone walks in who's dangerous or wants to hurt you, I can sense them and tell you. But I also don't know enough about anything or anyone in specific to cause them to want to kidnap me."

"Well, I guess that works." Brandy raised her glass, and the other two women held theirs up. Brandy raised an eyebrow at Diana.

"I can drink if there are no paying customers, and I don't get drunk. Mr. Hades has told me as much." Diana looked around. "And I don't see any paying customers."

Panterra and Brandy laughed as they clinked their glasses with Diana's.

After about 20 minutes, the three brothers along with their animals and Hades walked out of the room they'd been in. They all looked relatively unscathed. In fact, they were all smiling, and Hades patted the guys on the back before walking around to the back of the bar. "Diana, can you get us a bottle of Nestis?"

"Sure, I'll go grab it from the cooler." Diana walked toward the back of the room where a large wine cooler stood.

Brandy looked from Hades to the brothers, looking for some sign of damage or injury, but none of them were acting like anything had happened.

Before she could ask, Diana came back carrying a bottle of white wine.

Hades reached for it before Diana could open it. "This is our newest white, Nestis. Please let me know what you think." He opened the bottle and poured the seven glasses Diana had placed in front of him.

Diana gave each person a glass, leaving one each for her and Hades. After raising their glasses in a silent salute, they all drank.

"This is really good. I like it." Panterra was the first to finish her glass.

The brothers preferred beer, but when Hades gave you a new wine to taste, you taste it.

"Oh, it's a lot sweeter than I thought it would be. I like it," Brandy commented.

Both Panterra and Brandy looked at the brothers to gauge their reaction.

None of them grimaced, so that was a good sign. There had been times when the wine Hades had had them try out was awful at best. In his free time Hades really enjoyed creating new wine combinations, and not all of them worked out. Some did, like this white.

"I think you nailed it, Hades. This is good," Cee commented with both his brothers nodding in agreement. Even Diana was trying to get to the bottle for the last bit.

"I'm so glad you all like it. I created it for Persephone for when she gets home. It's named after her and everything." For being the king of the Underworld, Hades had a soft spot for her. It helped in some situations because ever since he met her, she had been able to calm him when no one else would dare try. She also took her responsibilities as the wife of the king seriously. In many ways she was the Queen of the Underworld, but no one called her that. Not around Hecate at least. Rumor had it she did have a crown, but she didn't wear it out.

After they finished the bottle and said their goodbyes, the brothers, animals, and two ladies turned to leave. As they were leaving, Basil, Hades corporate financial advisor, was arriving to the tasting room. Panterra turned to see Diana's face light up when she saw him.

"Good afternoon, Diana. I need to speak with Hades, and then I'll spend time with you," Basil told her as she came up to give him a hug.

"Hades, Basil, do you need me to stay?" Cee asked, as the vineyard's financial manager.

"No, it's not necessary at this point, but if it becomes so I'll let you know." Basil followed Hades back to the conference room they had all left just 30 minutes ago.

"I wonder what that was about," Jan commented as he walked toward the door, his phone in hand, hoping for a call. He had been told when the group reached where Meredith and the rest of the Dryads had camped, he would be called.

Not wanting to open a wound but needing to keep Jan out of his own head, Theo stepped away from Panterra and walked alongside Jan.

"Still nothing?"

"No, and I'm worried about not hearing from them yet. Does this mean they couldn't find the camp? If they did, are they just busy helping people? What's going on?"

"I don't know, but whatever is, we are here for you." Theo held back and waited for Panterra. When Panterra caught up, he held her up and let everyone continue walking toward the car. Coming to a stop, Theo turned toward Panterra.

"Are you busy right now?" Theo asked her in a low voice.

"Not specifically, the Reapers know what they're doing, and there's nothing in the near future that will need me to be available."

Ever since Panterra became the leader of a ward of Reapers, they had to work around her schedule. It wasn't as hard as it used to be now with cell phones and digital schedules, but it was still something they needed to be mindful of. It was a tradeoff for them being able to live together for the most part of the year.

"I need you to go and speak to your contacts and see if they've heard anything about the Dryads. I have a really bad feeling about this, and if Brandy is okay with it, I'd like you to take her and see if she can find anything out from her contacts as well. I want to know as much as I can before the call comes in because I have a feeling once it does, things are going to move fast. I don't like going into battle without knowing who my enemy is.

"Battle? Theo, what's going on?" Panterra yelled as quietly as she could while still showing her displeasure with what he was saying.

"Not now, we'll talk later." Theo and Panterra quickly caught up to the group just as they were reaching the car.

When they got home, Jan immediately went to his part of the house while the rest stayed in the main part and sat on the couches in the living room. Brandy stood and walked into the kitchen.

"Do any of you want anything?" Brandy opened the fridge and rummaged around looking for something to drink.

"Yeah, can you grab me a soda? Cee? Theo?" Panterra looked at the brothers.

"Nothing for me but thank you," Theo answered, but Cee was deep in thought.

"Earth to Cee? Is everything okay?" Brandy nodded toward Cee.

Without answering, Cee stood and walked toward Jan's wing.

Theo watched his back and shrugged toward the two women.

***

"Jan, we need to talk. Have you heard anything from Erato or any other the other Dryads?"

"No, I haven't. How long should I wait before going out there myself? I can't live without her. You know that."

"None of us can live without her. She's been with us for a long time, and none of us want anything bad to happen to her. But there's something more important going on right now."

"What could be more important than Meredith right now?

"We need to figure out if it's actually Set behind this, and if he is, what he is planning? You know about Meredith's stone, right?" Cee tentatively asked.

"Of course I know about her stone. Why should it matter?" Jan asked.

It had been years since Jan had helped the Dryads. Originally, they had nowhere to go. Meredith said she knew of a place, but it would take a long time to get there on foot. The brothers had talked about it and knew they couldn't keep the group of Dryads near the gate forever. After speaking to Hades, they agreed to let Jannes take Meredith to the location and make sure it was safe. If it was and the current occupants were okay with the Dryads at least temporarily living there, then Cee and Theo would assist the rest of the Dryads with using the portals.

"Oh! My Meredith, you have returned!" a small goblin yelled as he ran out of his rock house.

Jan saw Meredith shy away from him as he ran up. Trying to help, Jan reached out to her.

"Hello, I'm Jannes Cerberus, a guardian of the Underworld Gate. The reason I'm here is to request something of you on behalf of Hades and the Gods of the Underworld Committee."

"Meredith, who did you bring into my forest?" the goblin asked defensively.

"He's a friend. Please listen to him," Meredith implored.

"Fine, okay, so what do you wish of me, Cerberus?"

Jan spread his out hands. "We need of a location for a group of wayward Dryads. They are currently under the care of the Cerberus, but they need somewhere safe."

"How many and are they as pretty as my Meredith here?"

Hearing the remark, Jannes felt a tinge of pain in his chest. *What is this feeling, this pain?* "There are twenty including Meredith who will need a place to live."

Meredith glared at Jan. "Wait..."

However, his look stopped her thought.

Looking around, the Goblin counted something on his fingers before turning back to Jan. "Yes, I think I can accommodate that many, at least for a bit. Do they have a plan to relocate?"

"Yes, we plan on having a place set up which will become our final home," Meredith answered, without a second thought.

"Okay, then yes. It will be good for a bit at least."

"How soon will they be coming? I need to get everything ready." The goblin looked up at Jan.

"How long do you need? We can start bringing them here today."

"Okay, but you must not come to my house. Please arrive on the edge of the forest. I will have the toad fairies guide them to where I will have them stay." Before he bounded off, he grabbed Meredith's hand and kissed it. "Until later, my Meredith."

As Jan and Meredith walked away, he wanted to ask her what had happened and how she knew the goblin, but she didn't seem to want to tell the story.

"Are you sure you're okay with your sisters being here?" Jan asked softly.

Meredith shook her head slightly, tears glimmering in her eyes. "Yes, they'll be fine, but I can't move here. Please Jan, don't make me go back. I can't live with him again. He's so slimy and moist, most importantly he was handsy. I have no idea why, but he wanted me to be his wife or something, and he got touchy."

"Yeah, we can figure something out. Are you sure you're okay with them living there without you?"

"Yes, like I said, they'll be fine, but I won't go back there. Also could you maybe talk to him about how he needs to keep his hands off people." She grabbed his hand, turned, and moved through the forest.

When they reached the edge of the forest, Jan opened a portal to transport them back to the Gate. Jan looked down at her hand, and a small part of him burst with happiness before turning to pain. She won't like me when she finds out what I've done.

When they arrived, Hades and the brothers were engaged in conversation.

"He said he would allow them to stay with him. At least for a bit."

"That's good news. When can we start moving them? The Dryads are getting antsy about being here." Hades turned to Jan and Meredith.

"He said they can go now, but we can only deliver them to the edge of the forest. He will guide them from there."

"Okay Theo, do you want to gather up the Dryads and let them know what's happening?"

Nodding, Theo walked out of the room.

"Meredith, will you be able to guide your fellow Dryads to the house?"

"NO! I mean great Hades, I'd prefer not to, if you don't mind? Could I possibly stay here with you all?" She turned a slight pink in the cheeks at making the request.

Hades arched his eyebrow and looked at Jan, who just shrugged.

"I guess I can find something for you to do. I have a couple of businesses I own you could probably work at. But it will be hard work."

"Anything to not have to go back there." Her words edged her closer to Jan.

"Okay, we have a plan." Hades turned back to Cee and continued the conversation they'd been having.

"Well, I guess that was easy." Jan nudged Meredith before stepping forward.

***

Twenty minutes later, all the Dryads were standing in the cavern by the Gate. The women were discussing plans for what they were going to do now they would have a place of their own.

As they walked to the portal, a young Dryad turned to Meredith. "Miss Meredith, are you not coming with us?"

"Not right now. I have more to do here before I meet with you all. Know I am there in spirit." Meredith hugged the other Dryad. Meredith waited for the Dryad to walk toward the portal with Cee.

Over the course of the next hour, the brothers helped all the tree folk except for Meredith, who had stayed behind. When they were all gone, the brothers returned together.

"Well that's it. I would like to consider this a success. I hope they're happy," Cee added while he patted Jan on the shoulder before leaving the cavern.

"They will be. We feel more at peace with other trees, even if they don't talk." Meredith chuckled at her comment.

"Um, Meredith would you like to have dinner with me?" Jan asked, looking at the floor, afraid she would say no.

"Sure, did you even have to ask?" She smiled as Jan looked up at her. "You aren't used to having to ask people, are you?"

"Not really, but I feel I shouldn't demand dinner with you. You're not like the other people I normally spend time with."

Meredith looked around at Hades and Jan's brothers, who were pretending not to listen. "You mean like, a woman?"

"Yeah, something like that." Jan chuckled this time, gaining a red hue.

***

"Jan, come back. Where were you?" Cee shook Jan's shoulders.

"Just thinking about the day I asked her out to dinner. That night, I found out about her stone. I wonder if she even knew about it before I realized it."

"It's the stone I worry about. Between the stone Panterra gave to Sopek and the blue stone taken from Fenrir's forge, I wonder if it's the stones are the root of all of this."

"We know what the stone in Turk's collar could do. We don't know enough about the green stone Panterra traded for her freedom."

"Damnit Cee, what DO you know? Stop telling me what you don't!" Jan paced around his living room.

"I don't know yet, but I'm going to do some research into what the stones do, and what Set is trying to do."

Cee walked back to the other part of the house, leaving Jan willing his phone to ring.

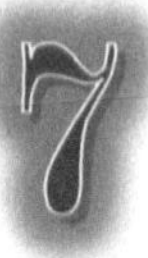

"So we know the blue stone assists in communication between planes. Can we think of what that means?"

The group was back in Hades conference room. With Persephone still at her parent's house, Hades couldn't leave the vineyard. Along with Cee, Jan, and Theo were Panterra, Brandy, Hades, and Fenrir.

After Cee left Jan, he started researching the stone which had previously been in Turk's collar. Looking over at the stone in Cleo's much smaller collar, he had realized it would be easier and faster to bring Fenrir into the group, since he was the one who had made the stone.

"Fenrir, my old friend, thank you for travelling here." Hades clasped Fenrir's forearm when he had arrived with Cee and Brandy earlier.

Fenrir briefly looked at Brandy. "I will help you as much as I can. After what happened in my forge, I will move earth to help you defeat who we are up against."

***

When Cee and Brandy had first travelled to Fenrir's castle, Fenrir had not wanted to help. He preferred to stay in his castle and mourn the loss of his apprentice who happened to be Brandy's brother Colin. After the fight in the forge, Cybele had taken Colin's body with her to mourn him. Without Colin or Cybele there, Fenrir was to the point of turning off the forge, which he had not done since faking his death.

"Are you worried about showing your face again since you technically 'died'? Brandy had asked as they were walking back to the portal after he had agreed to come back with them.

"No, I'm sure the cat's out of the bag about me being alive. It's been a long time, and this is more important than my life right now."

"We appreciate your help, for not only this, but also for Cleo's collar," Brandy said.

"I feel like I owed you after trading the stone for the much more powerful one. I feel like it's my fault Turk was lost."

"No, please don't think that. We were all tricked in one way or another. I don't fault you. If it wasn't for you, I wouldn't have met Brandy and would not have chosen Cleo as a companion."

Cleo wrapped her tail around Cee's calves as she performed figure eights while purring.

Fenrir reached down and pet Cleo. "She seems like a good companion, both her and Brandy." He smiled as he stood back up.

***

"So, what do we know about the stones?" Hades asked.

"We are still trying to figure out what the green one does, but the blue one we know. Do you want to explain what it does?" Cee motioned to Fenrir.

Fenrir started explaining the blue stone's powers.

When the blue stone was originally created, it was made to be able to communicate with different planes. While at the time, it didn't seem like a big deal. But the more Fenrir thought about it, the more it worried him. It had been commissioned right after the Titan Wars had ended. Over the centuries, Fenrir had thought more and more about the stone and what it could do.

"After looking at my notes from when it was first commissioned and with what we know, I think he's using it to communicate with Titans behind the gate."

"But why?" Brandy asked. Although she was relatively new, she had tried to learn as much as she could from Cee.

"I don't know, but it's the only plane he can't travel to. I mean he has access to the Underworld, and being a god means he can travel to the other planes without issue. I believe when the gate to the furnace was created, it was created in such a way the Titans wouldn't be able to communicate with sympathizers still on the earthly plane." Fenrir looked at Hades for confirmation.

"Yes, it was created at the same time as the gate to the Underworld. While the one to the Underworld dissuades communication between souls, it still allows Gods in and out. The one to the furnace was blocked off from even Gods. Only Reapers are allowed access in and out of the furnace. Well, it wasn't blocked originally. I guess we figured after the war, no Gods would want to interact with the Titans, but it appears that wasn't the case."

When the Underworld Committee created the gates, it was originally thought the Titans would realize the error of their thinking and could eventually be released back into the world. However, that's not what happened. Instead, the Titans continued to push their cause through sympathizers who were allowed to travel back and forth. After two smaller insurrections in a relatively short time, the committee decided it was best if the gates were closed for all.

"And that's the way it's been for a long time. We couldn't keep getting into battles over what was decided."

Perking up from watching his phone, Jan considered both Fenrir and Hades. "Do we know if Set had any other relationships with Titans? Could that be why he's doing this? But what does it have to do with Meredith?"

"We don't know if what's going on with Meredith is connected to all this." Hades tried to calm the eldest Cerberus.

"Bullshit, Hades. You know it as well as I do, and I want to know why? What's his end game?" Jan slammed his hand on the table before storming out the door.

"Hades, we do think it has to do with Meredith's heart. Why didn't you tell Jan?"

"Because I know what he would do if he found out, and we can't risk him going after Set, at least not by himself. Especially since this may be partially his fault."

***

Jan and Meredith had a good time at dinner. Since Meredith had wanted to stay and work for Hades, Jan had offered to let her stay in his room at their house while he stayed in one of his brother's rooms.

"You don't have to give up your room. I can sleep in the common room," Meredith told Jan as he was arranging hides for her on his bed.

"It's okay, truly it is. As you get settled here, we'll arrange for another place for you if you wish it. If you don't, you can stay here. We can always add another room to the house. There are perks to working for Hades." Jan chuckled as he finished laying the last hide on the bed.

"Thank you, Jan. Not just for letting me stay here, but for allowing my sisters to come back with you and helping them find a new place. You're a good person, Jan Cerberus."

If only she knew, Jan thought as he walked out of the room. She will only be here temporarily, he told himself, no need to tell her my past.

Over a month had passed since Meredith had moved in with the Cerberus brothers. Over time, Jan and Meredith became close, talking late into the night and walking into the Gate room together. All of their meals were together. Theo and Cee had discussed creating a new wing for Jan and Meredith as they both assumed it wouldn't be long before Jan moved back into his room. Neither Jan nor Meredith had talked about their past further back than when they met.

Now that she was accustomed to where they lived and the Gate, Theo thought it was time to have her talk to Hades about working. The next morning, Jan was waiting for Meredith to wake up. Theo and Cee had already left for the Gate and work. As Meredith walked into the common room, Jan did a double take. As Meredith looked at Jan and smiled, a dim red light could be seen coming through her thin shirt she had worn to bed.

"Good morning. Where's everyone else?" Meredith looked around the room.

Jan smiled. "They left for work already. Why don't you get ready?" Jan went back to what he was working on when she came out of the bedroom.

After she had freshened up, Meredith returned to the common room. She sat next to Jan, brushing her leg against his. "So, what's the plan for today?"

"I'll take you to Hades, and he'll decide what's the best job for you. With your skin color, it may be best if you don't interact with the common folk often."

Meredith looked down at her arms. She stood and walked back into the room without saying another word. All the way to the Gate, Meredith was silent.

What did I say? Jan thought.

Once they got to the Gates, Meredith walked away from Jan and straight to Hades. Jan lagged behind while Meredith asked Hades what she could do to help as well as if she could possibly get a place to live. Jan thought everything had been going well, but now with her asking about another place, he realized something must have happened, or Meredith didn't like him the way he thought he liked her.

"We can definitely get you a place. Is there something you're good at you could help with?"

"I can clean, and I can read. I can also do a bunch of other things, probably things you don't care about." She glared at Jan.

"What did you say? She's throwing daggers at you with her eyes." Theo came to Jan's side.

"I don't know. I just said she should maybe work in the back because of her skin color. I mean, was I wrong?"

"Not really, but do you think she liked you saying she shouldn't be around the public because she isn't traditionally pretty?" Theo answered, shaking his head.

"Wait, what? I didn't say that. I think she's beautiful. I just said her green skin may scare people. You know how it is with humans; they fear what they don't understand."

"Think about what you just said. Damn Jan, you screwed up." Theo laughed as he walked back to Cee.

As Meredith continued talking to Hades, Jan thought about what he had said to Meredith. As he watched her argue for the position, she wanted to work versus what Hades was offering, Jan realized he cared about her. He needed to tell her the truth about who he was, and what he had done. Even if it meant he lost her.

When Meredith was finished talking to Hades, Jan stepped forward before she could walk off.

"Don't worry, I'll be out of the house tonight."

Jan placed his hand on her elbow. "Please don't leave. I didn't mean what I said earlier. Well, I meant it, but not in the way I think you thought I meant it. You are one of the most beautiful women I've ever met. What I meant was your skin color isn't something people see every day and may bother those who aren't used to it. But now I realize it doesn't matter. The only things that matter is how you feel about yourself and how I feel about you. And you are the world to me."

Meredith blushed a little, which on her skin meant her normal green skin took on a burnt auburn coloring across the cheeks. She slid her arm out of Jan's grip and reached for his hand. For the next year Meredith and Jan dated while she worked for Hades, and he worked at the Gate with his brothers. Jan realized he had made a promise to always tell her the truth the day of their disagreement. However, he'd never told Meredith about his time as Commander, nor did Meredith tell him about the glowing red sphere in the middle of her chest.

Fenrir was deep in thought before he looked up at the group again. "Wait, how many stones does he have?"

Theo spoke up, "We gave Sopek a green stone for Panterra's freedom. We got it from Menninkainen, a goblin up in the Finnish forest."

"Was this the stone of Atlas?" Fenrir's attention was glued on Theo as he spoke.

"Yes, we believe it was, but I mean, there's no way to tell for sure. It was a large green stone, and Sopek wanted it. We didn't think anything of it at the time."

Fenrir leaned back and breathed heavily. "Hades, I think I know what he's up to, but I don't know for sure. How involved were you in the creation of the Gates?"

"I mean, I was the head of the committee, but I didn't actively do anything. I contracted you and Atlas to create the two, and that was pretty much the extent of my involvement. The particulars were handled by other members of the committee."

"Okay, so then let me start at the pertinent parts since we don't have all day."

As Fenrir started explaining, Jan's phone rang. Looking at the screen, he jumped up and walked to the door as he said hello. Everyone watched him until the door clicked close and turned back to Fenrir. Before Fenrir could continue, Jan returned to the room unphased. "Erato says the team has reached the encampment. She's going to call me when they have news."

Cee patted his shoulder as he sat back down.

"To begin with, there were two stones made, a green one to allow someone entry into the furnace and a red one that allowed someone to exit the gate. It was similar to the coins for the Underworld Gate."

Wait, is that why there are two coins? But we collect both? Jan thought. Does this mean we are forcing all of those souls everlasting time into the Underworld when we shouldn't have been? What have I been doing all these years? Did Hades know all this time?

"So, if you take into account the stone I made, the blue one allows for communication. If they were able to get all three stones together, they could open the Furnace back up," Fenrir spoke to the group.

"But if one stone allows for entry, and one for exit, they shouldn't be able to just come and go." Jan was trying to piece together the information. "I don't understand. Would a large enough group to come through to restart the war?"

"No one is looking at fighting right now, but your thoughts about the stones are a bit off. So, what's supposed to happen is someone uses one stone on one side, and then the other stone on the other. However, I believe if you have both stones on the gate at the same time, then you could bring down the barrier." Fenrir sighed and sank into his seat as the pieces finally came together.

"What barrier?" Cee asked.

"I got this, Fenrir." Hades stood and began pacing. "After the insurrections, and when the final Titan was found and put into the furnace, the committee agreed the best course of action was to create a barrier at the Gate. While before, Gods and Reapers could go in and out, the barrier made it so only Reapers could walk through. Even they had some issues we had to work around at the beginning. Eventually we had it set where they could leave once their soul was attached to a contract."

"So that's how they got the green stone and the blue stone. But what about the red stone?" Fenrir asked the group.

"It's Meredith! It was always her. I have to go now!" Jan ran out the door with Sammy on his heels.

Cee ran after him but before he could catch him, Jan and Sammy had vanished.

Walking back, Cee started to think about what he knew from before. With the new information, he figured he knew what Set was up to. As he stepped into the room, all eyes were on him. "He's gone. I assume to wherever Erato is."

Fenrir looked at Hades, puzzled by the sudden disappearance of Jan. "She is the red stone." Hades hung his head as he said it.

"What do you mean 'she is the red stone'?"

After a year of dating, Meredith asked Jan to join her in what had been his bedroom. His constant shadow followed him in. "Jan, I want to be with you, but there seems to be something keeping you from being with me."

"I really do care about you, but there are things you need to know about me." Jan reached for Meredith's hands as he spoke.

"Okay, I thought I knew everything, but what do you need to tell me?" Meredith looked up at him.

She is so beautiful, how can she love or even care about me after what I have done?

"Before I met you, before I became one of the Guardians of the Gate, I was the Commander of the

Gods military during the Titan Wars. I helped to direct forces to where they best could capture, and if needed, kill Titans."

Meredith looked at him. "Yes, but it was a long time ago. It's not who you are now, and I know this."

"No, well yes, I mean, I'm still the Commander when needed." Taking a deep breath, he continued, "Remember the morning I met you? In the field after the battle?"

Wary now of what he was about to tell her, Meredith sat on the edge of the bed, letting go of his hand as she did. Barely a whisper, she responded, "Yes, I remember that morning."

"I'd been asked by the Reaper to help collect souls. That much you know, but what you don't know is the battle was one of the final, and most decisive battles of the Dryad Wars. I'd been called in by the Underworld Committee to help them." Looking at her with tears in his eyes, he continued, "I stood by when I could have ended the war, but instead the Reapers led the attacks against the Dryads and other souls. I helped to kill so many, so many innocents. I don't deserve you, or anyone after the things I did."

Unsure as to how to respond, all she could think was to hold his hand again. The tears had turned into full crying has he knelt beside her with his head in her lap. She smoothed his hair back over and over and let him cry without saying anything.

After all his tears had dried, he looked at her. "Can you be with someone who has so much blood on his soul?"

"I can see the turmoil in your heart. I could the first day we met. Yet, you stood by us," she said, hand on his head.

"What? Absolutely, it was the just cause," he said, slightly confused.

"I can be with you, and I've always known I'd be with you. You're a good person who, at the time, did what you thought was needed. You can't blame yourself for the actions of others. I assume Cee and Theo were also involved? Do you blame them for the actions they took during the wars?"

"No, never, they were doing what I'd told them to do." Jan was on the verge of being defensive of his brothers.

"Jan, do you really believe they were not also fighting for what they thought was best? If you had told them not to fight, would they have still?"

Jan thought about it for a minute. "I honestly don't know. I mean Theo may have, but Cee, I don't know."

"See, this is what I'm saying. You three are who you are. You were meant to do what you did. If you believe the cause was just, then I believe you." She looked into his eyes.

"You may be right, but it's painful. When I close my eyes, I see those I have helped to kill." Jan seemed so lost when he looked at Meredith.

"Do you see the Reaper you killed to save me and the other Dryads?"

"No, he was going to hurt you. It was a justified kill."

"Knowing what you know now, would you have done the same thing?"

"A thousand times over, I would. He was going to hurt defenseless Dryads who did nothing except exist."

Meredith's heart hurt so much for Jan. A red glow continued to grow inside her chest. Soon it was bright enough to help light the room.

Jan looked up at her, his face reflecting some of the red.

"What's happening?" Jan asked.

"You have your secret, and I have mine. I'm not completely sure what it is. I know it feels like a stone, and I've had it since I became a Dryad. I know when I'm feeling strong emotions it starts to glow. Never like this though." Meredith smiled as she looked down at Jan.

"Can I... can I touch it?" Jan asked as he reached up to her chest. A low growl could be heard behind Jan. "It's okay Tal, I trust her."

"Yes, but be gentle, I believe the stone comes closer to the surface as the emotion is stronger."

"Does it hurt? Can you feel it?"

"Only when it glows does it feels warm, and the warmth spreads, but normally I can't feel it, and it doesn't hurt."

Jan reached up and touched the glowing spot on her chest. Instead of the smooth skin he expected, it was rough, stone like in texture and a bit warm. He couldn't determine if the stone was warm, or if it was Meredith. As he felt the stone, he felt Meredith run her hands up his shoulders into his hair. As he looked up at her, she leaned down and kissed him. Slowly, he leaned into her and pulled her into the bed. Jan's constant shadow, Tal slide out the door silently.

"Wait, so Meredith has the stone inside of her? I've never heard of this happening, and how do we know it's the right stone?" Fenrir sat up straighter.

Cee was the one who answered as Brandy and Panterra were whispering to Theo about something. "We obviously don't know if it's the stone allowing exit from the furnace. All we know is she gained life soon after the last Titan was captured by Jan. What I've been able to piece together is the Titan had hidden the stone in a tree and was then captured. Assuming the Titan was hiding the stone for a reason, it would make sense if this were the stone holding the power."

Fenrir nodded as Cee explained his thinking. "If that is the case, then Set or whoever is behind this will have to have the stone removed from Meredith's chest in order to use it."

Upon hearing that, Panterra turned to him. "Does she have to die? Is there anything I can do? I'm a Reaper, so I should be able to go into the Furnace, right?"

"I think right now we need to come up with a plan and not be overzealous." Hades seemed distracted. "Meredith has been missing what? A couple of days? And the gates must be watched. We don't know Set's plan yet so we must be vigilant on all sides."

Brandy looked at Cee and Panterra who both nodded at her before they stood.

"I can stay here if you need me," Brandy said, and Hades nodded in acknowledgement.

She turned to Cee. Hugging him, she looked up and kissed him. "Please be careful, my love."

Before he could respond, she went to Panterra and hugged her. "Be careful, and bring Meredith and the brothers home, please?"

Panterra could see the pain in her eyes. "I will do my best," Panterra tearfully responded as she reached for Theo's outstretched hand. The three walked out of the room along with Diego and Cleo. Brandy turned to Hades and Fenrir. "What can I do to help?"

***

As Brandy and the two Gods started to plan, Cee and the group walked out of the vineyard.

"Where should we go? It just doesn't seem right to sit around doing nothing. Maybe we should travel to the Gates of the furnace? And, you know, have a look around?" Theo said, joking yet dead serious.

Cee had been plotting the whole time Hades had been speaking. He already decided on the best course. "Panterra, you go to the Gate of the furnace along with Theo. I will go to Erato and see if I can find anything out there. You won't be able to call me from the gate since both gates are messed up. If you need me, you'll have to portal. Or, you know what you could do, you could send Diego through and have him communicate with Cleo. Cleo and I have tested our tether, and we can be quite a bit away from each other and still communicate. Likely not Gate to the Furnace away, but portal distance."

Theo opened a portal and Diego, Panterra, and he walked through it. Cee watched them until the portal disappeared before he unlocked his phone to call Jan.

"Jan, where are you? I need to come to you."

"She's gone Cee, she's gone."

Cee's heart dropped at Jan's words, hoping they weren't too late. "Jan, where are you? I'll come to you."

Jan gave him directions to where he was and hung up the phone.

Cee looked at Cleo before opening the portal. She slowly blinked back at him. While he didn't fight often, he brought out his mace in preparation for what he may face.

10

The scene Cee walked into churned his stomach. Fallen Dryads littered the ground as far as he could see. The sun had already set in this part of the world, and his vision had not yet adjusted. From where he was, the fire's eerie glow illuminated the endlessly staring eyes of a number of Dryads who had fallen near the rock ring. Knowing Panterra couldn't stop doing what she needed to, he would call another Reaper to come in and help the Dryads transition. If their death was chaotic enough, they would have to go to the gate, but if it wasn't, they could be transitioned by a Reaper. Seeing no immediate dangers, Cee put his mace away. Dryads were strong souls but as he looked around, the beautiful glowing orbs were angry and writhing in the air. They seemed like they were glitching. As he pulled out his phone, he heard a sob coming from a line of trees. He could see his brother, but the phone call was the most important thing at this moment.

The phone only rang once before a women answered on the other end. "Good morning. Shinigami noodle house. How can I be of service today? Will this order be take out or dine in?" The female on the other side said, preparing for the order.

"This is Cee. I need to speak to Shinigami."

There was a pause and a click before another voice harder than the first answered in Japanese. "Cee, long time it has been." This woman's voice sounded as she had been smoking for most of her life, and from what Cee knew of her, she had.

"I need some of your more seasoned Reapers. A group of Dryads was massacred and—" he paused looking around, "and things are bad and getting worse."

"Understood. Darling, send you location. A detachment will be enroute."

Cee complied with the voice's request. Before he could finish moving to his brother's side, Reapers began appearing, many dressed in ancient Japanese attire, including a few samurai.

Cee found Jan kneeling on the ground holding something in his hands.

"Jan, are you okay?" Cee reached down and touched Jan's shoulder.

Turning slightly, Cee saw Jan was holding a jacket he had given Meredith. Tears formed in both sets of eyes. While Meredith was Jan's wife, she had become a sister to Cee and Theo, and right now two of them were feeling the loss. Cee knew Theo and Panterra would take it hard as well.

"Jan, it's bad and the souls are chaotic. They can't remain. I'm sorry. We must get back to the gate before things get out of hand." Cee grabbed his brother's arm, lifting him to his feet. "I'm so sorry, but we'll find her."

Still carrying Meredith's jacket, Jan took out his phone, likely calling Erato to tell her what was going on. Knowing the power of the Dryads, Erato would likely send others to help those who remain rejoin with nature, but also to also minimize the destruction the errant souls could cause. Because of how powerful Dryads were, many may be able to reconnect and stay, but with the souls Cee saw, he was worried.

"Did you contact Erato?" Cee asked Jan when he had lowered the phone.

"Yes, she said she will gather the council and will be here soon. Do you think…" Jan paused, looking around. "Who are these Reapers?" Jan asked, raising his voice. Anger building.

"They are mine," said a raspy voice from the tree line. Both brothers looked even though they knew the voice.

Jan looked at the tall woman standing just over 6' 6" with long jet-black hair and the figure of an Olympic power lifter. Jan remembered her very well from the Titan and Dryad wars. She was his number one enforcer in the first and his worst nightmare in the latter. "Are they up for the task?" he asked coldly.

"Ah Jan, they are more suited than you, Dryad lover." Her tone was equally cold.

"Stop." Cee stepped in. "I know there is history between you two but this must be done, and Shinigami is well versed with chaotic Dryad souls."

"Yes, it would seem so." Jan stepped up to his full height, still dwarfed by the woman.

"Those days are far behind me." She softened her tone as much as the rasp in her voice would allow. "I understand this is different but, what happened? I have never seen so many souls so angry."

All three looked around and could see the scene was dissolving and one Reaper already lay dead on the ground, killed by chaotic souls. Cee could see souls bouncing around the toppled body.

"We're still trying to figure it out. Please do what you can but keep your Reapers safe. We do have Dryads coming in to assist as well. You will be okay, right?"

Shinigami nodded. "Things have changed. Jan, I heard you have someone close to you missing. Please let me know if there is anything we can do to help you. Now, if you need anything, I will be helping my Reapers."

Jan could only nod as she walked away.

Cee's eyes followed her as she went to talk to a Reaper before he turned back to Jan.

"What do you feel? Dammit Jan, you have been with her for centuries. You would know if she was gone, so stop feeling guilty." Cee placed both hands on Jan's shoulders and gently shook him.

"I'll stay. You go back to the gates and see if Theo and Panterra have discovered anything. Be ready, we might be coming to the Gate hot." As Cee said this, a soul brushed his arm.

***

The night was warm and beautiful. The group was larger this year than previously, thought Victoria. She had only really come to the gathering twice now and was even more excited this year. The Dryad gathering was something everyone looked forward to, and this year she was going to tell her love how she felt. Ever since her first gathering and she had laid eyes on the beautiful, twisted oak, she could think of no one else.

She remembered the dancing and the music lifting her above the clouds as she twirled and twisted. To the point she couldn't think of a greater calling until she saw her. She was dancing free in the firelight. All other light had vanished, and she just danced forward and back. Her hair was brown with streaks of green and gray. Her joining had been more equal, and the oak bark and the twist of her limbs reminded her of a twisted oak from before her first death.

Long did they dance together twisting and twirling until finally the fire grew low, and many of the others had moved off. They did not leave the glow but instead built their own. The two sat huddled together telling stories of days past and how they had come to be in this very moment together. After the final praises to the earth and the gathering had concluded, they promised to once again meet in one year's time at the great fire.

This was the night she was going to tell her how much she loved her. The last cycle had left her with a huge hole in her heart, and the sight of her beloved would fill the void with joy she knew.

She eagerly crossed the opening and stood feet from the great flame. The gathering had started, and dozens of familiar faces moved in on the fire. Some she knew from previous gatherings, and some she knew from rumor and stories. One such person crossed into the light whom she had only heard about. The soft olive skin was unique to her. She was said to have tamed the great warlord Cerberus brother and ended the Dryad war, saving their entire species.

Those thoughts quickly faded as she soon caught sight of the one she was so eagerly looking for, her twisted oak. They made eye contact and she smiled at her. Victoria's heart fluttered as they worked their ways around the fire. Just as they came within arm's length, her love fell into her arms. She held her, but something was wrong. She was not holding her back, and a new sound had erupted. It was not joyous, it was wrong. She looked around to see her family running in all directions, some falling, some screaming. She looked down at her beloved, who only stared back with empty eyes.

"I love you," she whispered as a pain seared through her back, into her neck, and then nothing. The two slumped to the ground, still clinging to one another even after death.

Cee jumped up from the ground and saw his brother and the Shinigami looking down at him. "Cee, are you ok? We thought the soul had killed you."

Shinigami looked out over the field and the scattered Reapers lying motionless on the ground. "It seems you are stronger than most."

"I saw the fire and the gathering, then they were attacked. Meredith was there. I don't really know what happened, but she was taken. She was alive when she was taken." Cee was exhausted.

Hope filled Jan's chest. "Then it's still possible. I'll make for the gate to prepare for the incoming."

Jan stood and walked a couple feet away from Cee before opening a portal. Looking back once more, he walked through still carrying the jacket, for what Cee could only imagine was comfort.

Turning, Cee saw a newcomer and he bowed slightly. "Erato, thank you for coming so fast. Please accept my and my brother's condolences. I am at your service."

Erato sadly smiled. "I wish this was under different circumstances, as having a Cerberus under my service would be a boon. However, as we are where we are, please tell us what we need to do to help my people."

Cee asked Erato to call the group together so they could organize and help the souls as quickly as possible. There was a lot even Cee didn't know about souls, especially those who were Dryads, Golems, and other natural elements.

"Everyone, thank you for coming. As you know, a group of Dryads were out here celebrating. As this yearly event is an open ceremony, not all of the souls will be Dryad. We only know of one missing while the rest have been killed. Please listen to Cee. Our goal is to help those who want to stay and those who are dangerous to move on to the gates."

As Cee looked around, he saw nods and tears from all who listened.

Hearing no questions or objections, Shinigami spoke up, "The first thing is to ensure each body as a soul. Since it just happened, most should still be tethered. It will appear as a wisp, or if you don't see a wisp, then they may still be hiding. When you find one, indicate it and a Reaper will come. Remember, these souls are confused and full of anger. They are dangerous but not because of malice. So, take care."

Everyone stood transfixed by her every word. The rasp seemed to hold the listeners even tighter. "If the soul wishes to remain then the tether to the body can be cut, and they can be free to join with an element again. The other Dryads will be here to assist. We Reapers are here to capture the souls who have given in and are a danger to the world." She looked around at the Reapers already at work. "Let strength and honor guide you!" She moved off with a detachment of Reapers and Dryads.

Cee was impressed by how she took control of the situation, and he knew they were all in good hands. Before moving to assist, Cee stopped by the fire and bent down. Two women were still clutching each other, lying motionless on the ground. "May you find happiness again," he whispered before moving on. Seeing them, Cee remembered when Jan first brought the Dryads to the gate all those years ago.

"What are they doing here, Jan?"

"They didn't have anywhere else to go right now."

"Yeah I understand, but why here? You know they are wanted, hunted, and generally not welcome anywhere," Theo interrupted Jan and Cee's conversation.

"And that's something we need to fix, not continue. They're no different than us, except their skin color is slightly floral versus our Greek complexion."

Jan let Theo and Cee continue to argue as he looked over the young women whom he had brought through. It was one of the first times a living being aside from a Reaper had been in the gate room, and Theo didn't know how he felt about it.

"Theo, Cee, I want you to meet Meredith. For the time being, she will be staying with us until I can contact other Dryads out there to help them. She is to be protected. Do you understand me?"

Meredith stepped forward, and Cee appreciated how she protected the others who were cowering from Theo's dog. He knew nothing would happen, but they didn't. It bothered him that he was troubled by this.

Cee's memory of the argument faded as he heard Erato calling his name. Remembering how the pain in Jan's eyes disappeared after Meredith came into their lives, he was worried about what would happen if she left them.

"Cee, I believe your…cat…needs you."

Cee looked for the portal only to find Cleo standing near Shinigami. It looked like they were having a conversation. The power Shinigami possessed was something Cee didn't know if she even knew the full extent of.

Seeing Cee was again paying attention, Cleo walked up to him before rubbing her face on his knee.

Panterra said Jan never came back to the Gate. She believes he has gone to the furnace and needs your help if you can pull yourself away from here.

"I was remembering something, but yes, let me check in with Shinigami. I believe I can come back with you."

"Cee, we're good. We have worked with the majority of the souls and just have the funeral pyre to create, which Erato is having her husband and the other men come to assist with building."

"Okay, then I'll leave, but please portal if you need my assistance. Thank you again for coming, Shinigami."

She smiled. "You know I could never resist you." She kissed him on the cheek.

Looking over the clearing one last time, Cee opened a portal, and he and Cleo walked through. As he appeared in front of the gate, Panterra and Theo rushed toward him.

"We must go now. Jan found Meredith, and they're at the Furnace gate."

Before Cee could say anything, Theo had opened a portal and was through it with Panterra close behind.

"I can't go." Cee stopped Panterra in her tracks.

"What do you mean?" Panterra said, wide eyed. "You have to come with us, right Theo?" Panterra looked at Theo for confirmation.

"The Dryads. I have to stay behind. It was so bad over there. The gate needs to be staffed. There's going to be a lot of loss today, so I need to help." Cee's voice was full of pain.

Panterra nodded in understanding before vanishing.

"Cleo, get a message to Shinigami, and let her know I'm here to receive. Then get a message to Hades and Fenrir and let them know what's going on. Things are about to get worse." Cee walked over to the stone desk and chair. They seemed so small and insignificant compared to was about to start coming in.

Jan came in about a hundred yards up the wooded hill from the Furnace Gate. Not wanting to make his presence known, he quietly approached the arch and moved from cover to cover. As he approached, a group of figures came into focus standing off to one side of the stone structure. Jan stopped at the tree line and found himself looking over a rocky field fifty yards from the group. So far, they hadn't noticed him, but he knew it would only be a matter of time before they did. It would happen sooner if he tried to cover the open ground.

From where he was standing, Jan counted seven individuals, all with their backs turned away from him. He believed some were male and some female. He didn't recognize any until his eyes rested on the smaller figure in the front. Jan felt the need to rush to Meredith, but even being a Cerberus, he knew he couldn't take on seven by himself. Especially if Set was among them.

Sammy leaned against Jan's leg as he took in the scene in front of him. He had not been to the gate separating the furnace from the rest of the known existence since the end of the Titan War. The rock structure looked exactly like the one back home. However, instead of a mist and runes welcoming souls, this one was dark. The stone seemed to absorb all the light around it while at the same time emitting a flickering red light like a fire burning off in the distance on a moonless night.

****

Jan stood looking the great stone archway towering over him like a giant maw ready to devour all who might stray too close. It was over, he thought. The great war had finally come to an end. He had personally seen to the last of the Titans being guided through into the darkness on the other side. He didn't really know what was over there. The few who traveled between the realms said it was like a great furnace. These travelers, or wardens, of this great prison were called Hel, or Reaper.

A figure strode up behind him to take in the view as well.

Jan looked over and recognized Set. "Welcome, Set, to the dawn of the new world, free of war and strife," Jan said, relieved.

Set stood looking up at the stone, yet his face showed a different story.

He must be heartbroken about all the Gods who died in the great war, Jan thought.

"This is not the end to war. It is just a pause, a brief break from bloodshed and tragedy. Heartbreak and longing will bring about another great war, and I foresee a different outcome." Set turned and walked off into the shadows.

Jan looked after him, brushing off the comment. "Ahh, we won. You should be celebrating," Jan called after Set who showed no sign of hearing the comment.

***

Mentally speaking to Sammy, Jan asked, Could you get closer without them noticing you and relay what they're discussing?

Maybe, I can try. This gate is similar to ours, and it's allowing me my glamour, which may help.

Okay, be careful.

Sammy maneuvered her way over to the group, walking a few steps before stopping and judging if they had heard her. Realizing they hadn't yet she continued moving, hunched over like she was a lion stalking pray on the African savannah. She continued moving from rock to rock until Jan lost sight of her about 10 feet behind them, obscured by a rock.

While she listened and Jan waited, he heard a soft woosh behind him. Grabbing his chakrams he turned, ready to disembowel whoever, or whatever, was behind him.

"Damn you're jumpy. You need to put those things away. If we wanted to kill you, then it would have already happened," Theo whispered as he plopped down beside Jan with Panterra and Diego both doing similar, making sure to keep out of sight from the group below.

"What are you doing here? How did you know where I was?" Jan asked as he placed the Chakrams back on his side.

When no one answered, Jan turned back to the group, forgetting he had even asked the question.

"Wait, if you're all here, who's watching the gate?" Jan looked from Theo to Panterra.

"Cee stayed behind. He said the Dryad massacre was bad," Panterra answered.

"It was. It was so bad." Jan shook his head.

"Don't worry, it's been taken care of." The stress sitting on his shoulders didn't lessen. If anything, it heightened because he knew he had to tell Meredith her family was dead.

Theo leaned forward. "What are we looking at? I see the Gate, but what are the people doing down there?"

"Meredith is over there, but I don't know why."

Squinting, Theo asked Jan how he knew.

"I have been with her for hundreds of years. I know her stance, and I know her mannerisms. Meredith's in the front."

Sammy came slinking back. After a brief period of quiet, Jan looked at the group.

"It's her, and it isn't good. They're saying she's the final piece, and with her heart it will finally open?" Jan looked at the group. "The stone. It must be the stone, almost like it's some kind of key."

Theo looked at Panterra and Jan before speaking. "I'm sure there has to be a key. It's a prison after all, but why are trying to release the Titans? It will cause another war."

"What do they mean about her heart? Why would her heart open anything?" Panterra glared at the group. She was still trying to catch up from Jan's comment.

"Her heart is a stone. Well, not her real heart. She has a red stone near her heart. She's had it at least since we met. We looked into it but never fully determined what it was or how she got it. We assume the stone was in the tree somehow when she merged with it," Jan said, not looking away from the group where one member was pacing back and forth.

What Jan hadn't told them was Sammy heard they were planning on ripping the heart out of Meredith, and there was no way he would allow that to happen. Even if it meant he would take them all on by himself.

Panterra had watched the exchange between Sammy and Jan when she had returned, and she knew it was more than just a comment about the heart being inside her. She hoped Theo had seen it as well because if she knew Jan as she thought she did, he was about to try a rescue.

***

A lull in Reapers gave Cee a chance to head back to the house for a minute before hopefully seeing Hades. Cleo had returned from the furnace with information, and he had an update for Hades.

Cee walked toward the winery and up to the boardroom where he could hear Fenrir and Hades talking. Before he could knock on the door, he heard Fenrir yell, "You have to tell the brothers."

Hades' response was so quiet Cee couldn't quite catch what he said, but thought it was something like, "It isn't time."

Cee walked into the room and saw Hades and Fenrir sitting at the table with the book between them and a bottle of wine sitting unopened on the table.

"Jan found Set. He's with a group near the gates to the furnace. Panterra, Jan, and Theo are staying near the gate. I don't know much more."

"Cee, do you know anything about the other stone?" Fenrir asked.

Cee looked puzzled. "You'll have to be far more specific. I've seen quite a few stones in my life."

Hades groaned and looked up from having his head in his hands. "It's her heart. She has a red stone near her heart."

Fenrir pulled a book from under the table. It was the size of a small journal, and Fenrir began flipping through the pages.

"You say it was red," Fenrir said, almost excited now.

"I just remembered Meredith telling me about it long ago," Hades said.

Fenrir flipped toward the back of the book and stopped. "I know what they're doing. To open the gate, you need the key, and I think her stone is the final piece. This is bad Hades. We are on the brink of another Titan War. You have to stop it."

"But how can they do that? I thought the gate was locked to all but the Reapers?" Cee was confused but eager for the information.

"It is, or at least it was. But there's a key. There's always a key, just like the one over there by the falls," Fenrir shouted.

"Has there been a reason for why yet? Why open the Furnace? It's been thousands of years." Cee mentally counted the centuries having passed.

Hades and Fenrir looked at each other before Hades answered.

"We still don't know."

"Okay. So they want to open it. How do they do that?" Cee moved closer to the table.

"By using three stones," Fenrir read from his journal.

Hades answered, "The blue stone is the key from the inside, transported there by the very wardens who guard the doors. The green stone allows for communication between the two realms. The red stone is the key from our realm. The keys have to be used at the very same moment. When working together, it will unlock the gate. If that happens, then the Titans will be released into the world. Unless they have changed for the better, which being stuck inside hell for centuries, I fear they may have changed for the worst, there will be a war."

"How do you know this?" Cee looked between the two elder gods.

"Because after Fenrir and Atlas created the gates, I and Set were the two responsible for getting them to work." Hades placed his head back in his hands. "We shouldn't have done it this way. But this was never meant to be a permanent solution. It was all just temporary. How did we lose our way so much? She was the guide..." Hades trailed off into another place.

"You had no other choice, then or now Hades." Fenrir placed his hand on Hades' shoulder. Bringing him back.

"With the third stone, Set will have to extract it, which means she will die." Hades stood and walked out of the room.

"There is much to do, Cee, for if we cannot stop them, we must prepare for war," Fenrir said, also standing.

"Thank you, Fenrir. I need to return to the Gate since more Reapers will be coming in soon." Cee left the winery, his mind in a stir and eager to start the unraveling.

13

"Okay Sammy, I need you to go back out there. We are going to move on Set. You'll be our lookout," Jan said, creating the plan.

Sammy slowly made her way over to the rocks near Set. While she sat there, Jan turned to talk to Theo and Panterra.

"Okay, while Sammy is gathering more information, I have a plan to get Meredith back. That should, and is, our main priority."

Theo nodded, but Panterra was deep in thought. "Jan, we need to prepare for more than just rescuing Meredith. I think Set is trying to open the gates."

"I understand, but I think if we do one, we can stop the other. We rescue Meredith." Jan eyes glowed a bright green when he turned to Panterra.

Panterra nodded in understanding. She still felt his single mindedness was misplaced, but he was a Cerberus, and the commander and warlord of the great war. It was her job to listen and obey. Even though the plan was to save Meredith, Panterra was prepared to do what she needed to as a Reaper if needed. There could not be another war.

Jan leaned in again. "Ok this is the plan. Theo and I will stand up and rush down, killing every breathing being we can. Panterra, your responsibility is getting Meredith to safety. Once you are clear, we will be close behind. I don't know if we can kill Set, but if we can save Meredith then his plans will be stopped, and Hades can follow up with Set."

Theo looked up and smiled. "I do believe, big brother, this is the best plan you've ever had." Theo's eyes began to burn a blue flame.

Just as they were set to stand, a familiar sound filled the silence, and a new member joined the group. Hades stood before Set, dressed for war.

****

After hearing everything Hades and Fenrir knew about the gate, Cee knew he had to figure things out. Maybe there was another way to stop the coming tide. Cee had made it back to the gate and was sitting at the desk, stacking and restacking 10 coins on the table over and over. They were told the coins power the gate. Powered the gate he thought. What if they unlocked the gate? His train of thought was crushed as a familiar voice filled his head.

"Cee, what's wrong?" Brandy could see in his absent stare something was weighing on him.

"My job is what's wrong. My life, all our lives. I have always prided myself on knowing what others don't, and now I feel like a kid lost in a library with no books." Cee slammed the smaller coin pile sending seven coins scattering across the floor.

"What? That's ridiculous. What are you talking about?" Brandy said, not quite knowing what to say.

"It's a long story, century's old. I just want you to know how much I love you. If something is to happen to me, make sure you understand I truly love you."

"First, you are scaring me. Second, where are Jan and Theo? And third, what could happen to you? Cee, what are you not telling me?" Brandy stood with her hand on her hip, daring him to not answer her.

"They're at the furnace. I don't know what could happen, but it looks bad. With what I heard from Hades and Fenrir, it could be really bad." Cee took Brandy in his arms and kissed her.

"We'll find a way to get through." Brandy kissed him hard. Cee looked at her and smiled before he sensed another person had joined their little party. He glanced over her shoulder to the waterfall and noticed a black clad Reaper walking in with a bag in his hand.

***

"Hades?" Panterra had noticed the new member of the party stepping through a portal.

The two brothers looked intensively now at the goings on at the furnace. Bits and pieces of the conversation drifting far enough for them to hear.

"…What are you doing…war came to an end long…" Hades said standing tall over Set.

Hades had arrived in his battle armor. The armor was golden with silver inlays. The brothers had always found it too pretty for war. Hades' helmet was obscured from view under his right arm, and his left hand rested on the hilt of his sword.

"Why…you have no…are due the freedom that…" Set responded arms crossed.

"…Agreement…Meredith…with me." Hades pointed at the imprisoned woman.

"…you are the…agreed." Set motioned for the female to be brought forward. The hidden three could see each other's confusion.

Hades nodded and stepped forward to take her arm.

Jan saw it first. A blade so fast only the flicker of the fire reflecting off it caught his eye. He watched as Hades dropped to the ground, blood flowing from a gash just under the protection of his gilded armer. His helmet dropped to the ground as he fell to his knees desperately trying to stop the flow.

"Now I will be the Lord of the dead, my dear Hades." Set was laughing as he walked over to Meredith, bringing the blade to bare again.

As the blade danced, the world slowed, and the stillness erupted into chaos. Theo had already left the cover when he saw Hades drop. He was a blaze of blue streaks as his blades contacted the closest of Set's followers.

Panterra was not far behind Theo, slicing the next down, and on to the next when she saw Meredith's body fall. Set outstretched his hand, which now held a brilliant red stone still dripping with blood. Her body didn't fall far as Jan slipped in, catching her before she found the Earth.

Time seemed to return as Set jumped back, realizing his men had fallen. He turned toward Jan while stepping back toward the shadows.

"There is no escape for you. I will finish what I started a thousand years ago. The Titans will be no more when I am done." Jan's face was flushed with anger, and nothing but vengeance was on his mind.

He laid his wife on the ground and stepped toward Set. Before he could get far, a new shadow caught his eye. He followed the movement as it moved between the flickering light to stand over his beloved. He realized too late what the shadow was.

The Reaper had been given one job by Set. He would see it through. As a reaper Sasha never liked the fanfare Set demanded, nor any of Set's cronies. He preferred to stand on his own. He watched as the group talked and talked. Set promised him riches and a future, so even though he didn't enjoy what Set was doing, it was worth it in the end. *So much talking and meeting just get it over with,* he thought.

Then before he could walk from his shadow, a newcomer appeared. He knew who this was; it was Hades. He did not fear many Gods, but Hades and his dogs gave him pause. Sasha slinked back into his hidey hole and watched. As he watched the moments unfold, he saw his charge fall toward the ground. "Yes, it's time." He moved from shadow to shadow.

As he neared, more and more of his enemies appeared, blocking his way. He stopped at the last shadow awaiting an opening. Then it came. The oldest dog set the woman down. Now. He swooped in, collecting the emerging soul and was gone.

"No!" yelled Jan as he saw the Reaper collect her soul. He knew he was headed to the gates. In a moment of hesitation, Set vanished and left Theo, Panterra, and Hades alone with Jan, an emotional wreck.

"They took her soul. We have to stop him. Panterra, to the gates with me. Hurry," Jan yelled, opening a portal. Before she could react, he was gone. She looked at Theo looking at Hades, whose bleeding had slowed with Theo's help. She said, "save him" before she opened her own portal and left.

Theo nodded, took Hades in his arms, and opened a portal of his own. As the group vanished, the wind regained command of the scene and blew dust over the fallen, threatening to bury them. The wind whipped freely until a figure stepped out, blood dripping from his fingers. Set had watched them leave. The plan had not gone as smoothly as he had wanted, but he looked down at the stone. The mission was still a success. As long as Sasha carried through with his part. He walked toward the furnace, ready for the next step.

Jan was rejoicing at the end of the Titan conflict in his war room and reminiscing about the Titans they had captured. However, a commotion stopped the small festivities.

"How can I help you?" Jan looked up from his command desk to see a tall, dark-haired man walking toward him.

"You can help me by telling me who sent Themis to the furnace," the man commanded.

"I don't know who you're talking about. You will have to be clearer. Not to mention, as you can see, I'm busy."

Two men came in and stood at attention. As one of the men looked over at Set, Set could see there was a slightly blue glow to his eyes.

"Ahh Theo and Argus, perfect timing. I need you to go to the northern quadrant and see if there is anyone still hiding out there."

"Yes, Commander Jannes," Argus responded while Theo just nodded. As they turned away, Theo looked back at Set and thought about staying around to see what he had to say, but he followed his commander's order. And he knew his brother could handle himself.

Set cleared his throat as Jan was still looking over the map.

"Oh, you're still here?" Jan looked up from the parchment. Jan had no time to deal with people who weren't helping.

"Do you know who I am? I asked you who sent Themis to the furnace." Set stomped his foot down near the table, shaking a few of the figures showing Gods or Titans on the battle map.

"No, I don't. And as I told you before, I have no idea who it was, so please excuse me. I have things to do. As you should know, we are cleaning up the remaining Titan resistance, so please come back later."

"No, you will answer me. I am Set, the leader of the underworld."

"No, Hades is the leader of the underworld." Jan moved the figures back into place.

"He may be the figurehead, but I am the one who actually does everything." Set crossed his arms as if to challenge Jan.

In hopes of appeasing this man who Jan realized was a god, he took a different approach. "I'm sorry Set, but I'm unsure as to whom you are referring to. I don't remember the name. But I have sent so many to the furnace it's hard to remember now," Jan said, pleased with himself.

Set was taken aback by the man's callousness to the people they had imprisoned.

Disgusted with him, Set held back his temper. "She was a Titan who was in the South Forest. She would have had a red stone with her."

"Let me call my record keeper in, and he'll look through the records. What's your purpose with her?" Jan was suspicious of what was going on and did not want to bring attention to the fact his brothers were involved.

"That is none of your business. Go call your brother in. This needs to be resolved now," he said, letting his anger get the best of him.

Jan called Cee in from the library and told him to bring the Titans registry, the book Cee had created to track the condition of the Titans in the war. Cee walked in with a heavy book, looking between Jan and Set.

"Commander, what's the name you wish for me to find?"

"Set, here, is asking about a Titan named Themis who is in the furnace apparently and may have been in possession of a stone. Can you please give me some information about her?"

"Yes, Commander." Cee flipped through the pages, running his finger down rows and rows of names.

"Can't you go any faster?" Set directed toward Cee.

Without responding to Set but looking at Jan for guidance, Jan waved him to continue searching.

"Here she is, Commander. It looks like she was taken from the Southern Forest after a brief chase. Oh, that's interesting."

As Cee was talking, Set was moving closer and closer to the book, in hopes of reading what Cee was.

Jan stepped between Cee and Set. "What is it?"

"It appears you took her in actually, and it seems she was with child."

As soon as Cee said it, Jan remembered. "Yes, I remember now. She put up a stiff resistance, strong willed for sure."

Set paced. "And the stone?"

Jan spoke up before Cee could, "She did not have anything besides the clothes on her back."

Set stepped forward. "Are you sure? No bag at all."

Cee skimmed over the record again. "No, there's nothing. If you want —"

Jan stepped over and shut the book before Set could start reading. "I assure you she had nothing else. Will that be all? I need to get back to my duties."

Set started to go after the book when Hades walked in.

"Set, what are you doing here?"

Stepping back from Jan and Cee, Set clasped his hands in front of his body while looking at Hades. "I was checking on something, but your Commander and Record Keeper were able to answer my question."

"Was it important enough to leave the Underworld?" Hades looked toward the brothers who just shrugged their shoulders.

"No Hades, I guess it wasn't." Set looked at the ground

"Then you should get back there before anything happens." Hades looked at Set until he turned and left. When he knew Set was gone, he turned toward Jan and Cee.

"What did he want to know?" Hades asked, curious as to why his second in command was not where he had left him.

"I sent a Titan to the furnace. He was questioning why she was there, and if she went with a red stone. She didn't have it on her."

"Why?" Hades asked. Again, the brothers shrugged their shoulders.

"Jan, may I return to the library?" Cee asked, anxious to return to his studies.

"Yes Cee, you can go back to your books." Jan watched Cee walk back to the library before turning back to Hades.

"I don't trust Set. He was asking about a red stone Themis supposedly had on her. When I came upon her though, she didn't have it. He seemed more interested in the stone than he did her. Why was a god of the Underworld so interested in what a Titan had in her possession?" Jan thought out loud.

"I don't know, but when you get a chance, have Cee look into it. Watch your back Jan, especially if he finds out you were the one who sent her to the furnace." Hades patted Jan's shoulder before walking out.

As he was leaving, Jan responded, "He already knows it was me."

Cee approached the Reaper as he walked toward the gate. "More souls from the Dryads?"

The figure nodded, not making eye contact with Cee.

Brandy watched from the other side of the small desk when she saw Jan burst through the falls, Panterra on his heels.

Jan looked around like he was confused or searching for something.

Brandy waved at him. "Hello Jan, Panterra, you have news?"

In that moment, Jan's eyes found the Reaper, and the Reaper knew his ruse was discovered. He sprinted toward the gate, bag outstretched.

Jan was also enroute and closing on the black clad figure.

Jan's blades appeared in his hands as he reached out to the figure catching him just under the shoulder blade, sending him forward into the stone gate.

He fell hard to the floor, covering it with blood. His hand was buried in the small leather bag.

Jan stepped over his foe but paused as he saw the soul freed of the bag. His moment of hesitation gave the dead man his success.

The coin came out and activated the gate. With grace and beauty, Meredith's soul glided through the gates and out of the world of the living. At that moment, two lives disappeared.

"No!" Jan screamed, grabbing the limp body of the Reaper, tears welled in his eyes when he realized she was gone.

Cee ran to his side.

Behind him, Panterra had fallen to her knees crying, her face buried in her hands.

Brandy had made it to Panterra's side and was consoling her, still not realizing what had happened.

"She's gone, my love." Tears flooded down Jan's cheeks. Still holding the body, he threw it across the room. As it hit, a clinking sound grabbed his attention. Lying on the floor were coins. Gate coins discarded and scattered over the polished floor. He looked over at the desk and saw the same glint.

Cee was saying something, but Jan wasn't listening. He walked over to the desk and grabbed the remaining coins. Without saying a word, he returned and stood in front of the great stone arch.

He felt a tug on his pant leg and looked down to see Diego. Jan patted his companion on the head. "I'm sorry, but I can't live without her." Without another thought, Jan activated the gate with one of the coins he collected and followed his wife.

16

Walking through the gate, Jan was immediately in a large field with trees, grass, and a flowing creek. He could see the ripples as the water trailed past the small stones. All around, singles and couples walked. The temperature was not too hot, nor too cold. In Jan's mind it was perfect weather, an ideal day. Looking around, he walked toward Meredith sitting next to a tall woman. A sense of familiarity flashed through Jan's mind.

Seeing him, Meredith jumped up and ran to him. She seemed to be almost translucent, there but not there at the same time, like a whisp.

"Jan what are you doing here?" She stopped just out of reach.

"What do you mean what am I doing here? You're my wife. I wasn't going to let you die and not do everything in my power to be with you. And if being with you means my own death, then so be it." He stepped toward her, but her reluctance made him stop.

"But did you leave Theo and Cee at the Furnace?" Her face looked concerned.

"Yes, and they can handle themselves. My life is with you, be it on earth or here. Don't you understand? I can't be without you." His eyes welled with tears.

"Jan, I can't ask you to do that. Your place is among the living, and my place is among the dead." She stepped back, toward the unknown woman.

"No, it isn't. My place is with you, and I will say it again be it living or dead. Since you died, my place is with you among the dead."

Jan burst forward, wrapping Meredith in a hug, tears flowing, not just at the thought of losing her, but because the mass of emotions overwhelming his system. Jan knew Meredith had saved him, in more ways than one, and he just needed her now.

Slowly, Meredith extracted herself from Jan's grasp and reached for his hand. Taking it, Meredith turned to the woman.

"Not exactly," entered a new sweet, exotic, yet familiar voice.

Jan looked past his wife. "What are you talking about? No one comes back from the gate. No one." Jan's words lacked confidence. Another time and another story of another brother came to his mind.

"You need to listen to what this lady has to say. I think a lot of the questions we have may be answered," Meredith spoke softly, bringing Jan's defenses down.

"What questions?" Jan said, looking at his wife.

"Jan, she knows. Just listen to her."

"Hello, I am Janus Cerberus," Jan said without knowing why.

"Jan, please. You don't think I don't know you, Cee, and Theo? How I have not wished to see you with my own eyes? Every time a new soul comes, I hear your voices. It pains me to have left, but I had to. It would have been different if Hades would not have failed in his mission and failed to fulfill the promises he made to me when the gates were activated." She crossed the field, stopping next to Meredith.

"Oh Janus." Reaching up, the woman ran her hand over Jan's cheek. "I have missed you so much."

Stepping back from her touch, Jan couldn't find anything to say.

She softly chucked yet her eyes betrayed the laugh with sadness. She responded, "No, it has been a very long time, and so much has changed. You wouldn't remember. I am known here as Minthe, but you can call me something different? I can see the lost look in your eyes my son. Jan, you and your brothers were a part of my soul just as Hades was," she spoke.

"What? I remember your face, but as a shadow, a glimpse in the wind." As he said it, the darkness in his mind receded and it came back. "Mother," Jan whispered, and Meredith gasped.

"Yes Janus." Her emotions starting to show.

"But why are you here? Surely you didn't choose this fate," Jan said almost frantically.

"Actually, I was telling Meredith the story when you surprised us," Jan's mother said, sitting back down.

Meredith sat back next to Minthe while Jan stood behind unmoving, unsure what to do, yet he held Meredith's hand like a vice, unwilling to let her go.

"So, I assume by now you know how the great gates work or at least, should have worked," Minthe said with a tinge of anger.

"Not so much. Cee has been trying to research as much as he can, but there are some aspects of our history that comes up empty."

"Interesting, I assumed they would tell you everything. As you are a Cerberus."

"Who is they?" Jan asked, already sensing the answer.

"Well Zeus, Hades, Set, any of the elder gods obviously." She looked at him sideways.

"No, in fact Set is why many are here today, and specifically why Meredith and I are. He's trying to open the gates to the furnace." Jan squeezed Meredith's hand even tighter.

"He has always been such a rat." Minthe's hands fisted, and she pounded her thighs. "I knew we could not trust him, but Zeus and the others felt he should be included. I don't know why, and I never got a chance to ask, nor would they have likely told me." Her shoulders drooped.

Minthe began her story.

***

Ares, Fenrir, and Zeus were standing around Fenrir's work bench when Minthe walked in.

"Good afternoon, is there anything I can bring you?" Minthe asked as she walked up to the men.

Their hushed discussions stopped when they turned toward her.

"Nothing I can think of. Thank you, Minthe." Ares replied as he turned back to look at something on the work bench.

"Nothing here either, but may I ask you something?" Fenrir replied.

"Anything."

"Do you believe someone would willingly sacrifice themselves for the betterment of the world?"

"Is it something that truly benefits the world, or is it something benefitting the few under the guise of the whole?"

"Just tell her, Fenrir. I tire of word games." Ares rubbed his eyebrows with his hand.

"If someone was sacrificed to complete the gate to hold the Titans back for an eternity, do you think someone would willingly give themselves?"

"I am sure many would, to stop this war. I would," Minthe answered.

"No Minthe, we are not asking you to do that." Fenrir put up his hands.

"No, you aren't, but my answer is still the same."

"But what about your boys?" Ares asked.

"They are on their own, and sometimes it seems they don't remember me anyways. But to end the war of all wars and save my boys? If I could end the war and ease the torment inside Jan just a little, I would."

"Wait, you willingly gave yourself for what? What did your death do to save us?" Jan was exasperated.

"As I am sure you know now, to open the gates to this wonderful world, you need death. It's not the act of dying but the unbelievable unleashed power inside the soul. In secret we built the gates, one could not be without the other. This place was created to power the other. Here, wayward souls can calmly frolic and be at ease, so one day they can return to your realm, hence the coins. But while here they power the gates of the furnace, the fiery prison of those who did evil upon the world.

"But you have been here for what seems like a millennium," Jan said calming his own soul.

"Yes, that was not supposed to be the way. Why are no souls returning as they should? They are to come with a coin, yet no souls pass with a coin," Minthe asked, looking at Jan the gate keeper.

"What do you mean they were supposed to return? We keep the second coin. One to power the gate the other in a drawer."

Minthe looked at him puzzled.

"Them returning was part of the plan, what has Hades done?"

***

"So, what will happen to me?" Minthe asked Fenrir.

"From best we can tell, you will pass, and your soul will help power the gates. The one to hold the destructive souls and the gate for the Titans. And once you are there in that world, then you will be the gate keeper on the inside. Keeper of the stones."

"What then?" Minthe asked.

"As Hades' wife, your job will be to protect the new souls, to help calm and teach them how to transition back to the world of the living. Once they are ready, they may return." Fenrir moved objects from one hand to another nervously.

"When will I be able to return? Will I be able to return?" She asked.

"We don't know, but someone must always be there as a guide."

"Thank you, Fenrir. You have always been a good friend." Minthe gave him a tight hug. "In case I never see you again," she whispered in his ear.

***

"Wait, so you just left us? With who?" Jan said.

"Left you? You were fighting a war, and I had to do my part so you could win. Or was it all in vain? I was an elder god, and the gates needed the power of my willing soul."

"Who was our father?" Jan asked point blank.

"What? You don't know who your father is?" Minthe muttered something under her breath too quietly for Jan to hear.

"No, souls transitioning sometimes forget their old lives, but if I was born who I am, then I must have a father."

Meredith looked up from her thoughts. "Why does it matter, any of it? We can't leave."

"But you can. The coins open the portal on the outside and in here."

Jans hand was shifting the coins back and forth in his pocket.

"I don't know why, but grabbing the coins before I went through the gate felt like the right thing to do." Jan lifted the two coins from their concealed hiding place and held them up.

"So, these coins are like ferry transport, but instead of a ferry, it's a gate. The Titan gate is not the same; instead of coins, the key is the stones." Meredith said looking at Jan.

"My gate works when a Reaper collects a soul. The power of their soul is syphoned and condensed into two coins. One coin is used to power the gate on your side. The other coin was to travel with the soul to me."

"So, the second coin, wrongly taken from the soul at the gate is their key back to the world of living. They should be traveling with it. IT SHOULD NOT BE LEFT IN A DRAWER, WHAT EVER A DRAWER IS!"

"I always wondered why there was 2 coins." Merideth looked at the coins in Jan's hand.

"After sending so many through the gates, I just couldn't look beyond my own nose anymore. I think without my companion and Meredith, the world of the living would have nothing to offer me. You have no idea how much the world has changed." Jan was frustrated about the lies he never cared to uncover.

"Companions?" Minthe looked between the two.

"At some point, Cybele gave Hades three collars with different stones which allowed us to speak with a companion animal. Theo and I have always had dogs, but Cee is on his second cat."

Minthe considered what Jan had just told her. "Of course he is. And they help you?"

"More than you can imagine. Not only do they help at the gate, but they are always there if we need something. Sammy." Jan eyes teared.

"I take it Sammy is yours?"

Jan knew she had no idea what he was saying but described the animals anyways. "Yes, I have Sammy, she is a boxer dog, Cee has Cleo the cat who is a Maine coon, and Theo has Diego, a bull mastiff."

"Do they live forever?" She cut in.

"Sadly no. In fact, Cee recently lost his dog, Turk, and it really hurt all of us."

"Interesting." Minthe sat back down on the rock. "It would seem like nothing stayed the way it was supposed to be." She fell silent.

"Mother, you must explain the rest. I must return with Meredith to help my brothers."

"The souls were to return to the mortal world when they were ready. This was the plan all along. The point of the war, all the sacrifice, Titans, Gods, this was the place the compromise, the promise to the souls lost." She trailed off into thought.

"So what do we need to do to return?" Jan asked.

"Take one of the coins and put it in your hand, then place your hand on the gate. Jan, you will return in the form you see, however Meredith will not. She will be a loose soul that will need to merge again."

"Come back with us. You could, I have all these coins."

Minthe looked at Jan with tears in her eyes. "My place is here. I still believe in what we built. My purpose was to save these souls. She lifted her arms wide over her world.

Jan looked out and really saw for the first time. Everywhere, there were souls everywhere.

"I need to be here to help those who wish to return. Please tell Cee and Theo I love them, and I want them to be happy. Meredith already told me about them and how they have found love. It makes my heart happy to know. It's okay. I'm needed here, but you need to stop Set from opening the Furnace gate. If the gate is destroyed, I don't know what will happen to this place."

Jan and Meredith both thanked and hugged Minthe. Handing Meredith a coin, Jan took a coin in one hand while holding her hand in the other. "Ready?"

Jan led her to the gate hand in hand. "Can you make sure I merge with something attractive? If you end up like that toad dude, we're done."

For the first time since being here, Merideth smiled.

"Yes, anything for you, my love." Jan kissed Meredith's forehead as he closed his eyes and held the coin to the gate. Behind him he heard the last words "Your father is Hades."

When he opened his eyes, both hands were empty. Frantically, he looked around. Panterra stood there and rushed to Jan.

"You're back. Oh, my gods you're back! Meredith, her soul returned as well but how?" Pantera was talking so fast.

Jan quickly hugged Panterra. "I'm fine. Where are Cee and Theo? They were here, weren't they? I have to go do something. Can you tell them to meet me at the winery?" He ran through the waterfall.

"Meredith? Where is she?" Pantera pointed toward the waterfall.

Panterra shrugged before creating a portal to the furnace to tell Cee. She already knew Theo was there with Hades.

Jan found Meredith's wisp bouncing near the water. He made as much noise as he could to alert her, not knowing what she may or may not hear, if anything. As he approached, he noticed the wisp turn around and turn a light shade of purple before bouncing off toward the trees. Running to catch up, Jan felt almost as if they were playing tag, Meredith letting him get closer before bounding off again. He laughed as she launched herself toward a small copse of Pacific Madrones she loved to visit whenever she came to the Gates.

Seeing the wisp jump from tree to tree, Jan already knew which one she would pick but waited for the wisp to make its way over to a sapling. Meredith had liked the tree ever since they moved to Oregon. With reddish bark that peeled away to show a coppery under bark, Meredith often commented on how the red and copper were so pretty. It was no surprise Meredith was drawn to the trees in her wisp state. As Jan watched, Meredith's wisp circled the tree a couple of times before she slowly started to merge with the sapling.

As Jan watched, the tree shrank and grew arms and legs. Where once were branches and leaves, were now hair and limbs. He stood still until Meredith took her first step toward him. When she did, he knew the merging was complete, and he rushed to take her in his arms. Brushing the red hair away from her face, he kissed her and hugged her tightly again.

"Jan, I can't breathe. Let me go." Meredith's voice was but a squeak into Jan's chest.

Reluctantly releasing her, Meredith stepped away before looking down at her new body. "Well, I guess I'm going to have to get all new clothes. The old ones were for someone with green tinted skin, now I'm just tan."

"Now is not the time to joke Meredith. I almost lost you, and I still could if we don't stop Set."

Meredith reached for Jan's hands. "If not now, when Jan? We must find humor and love when we can, not when it's the right time."

Looking at her bright green eyes, the color of the leaves in the spring, Jan nodded. For too long he took her love and her presence for granted. If they came through this alive, he vowed to never take her for granted again. Taking her hand, he walked back to the Gate.

"I can't wait to see what Brandy and Panterra think of my new look. Maybe I should die every couple of hundred years so I can get an updated look."

Stopping at that comment, Jan looked like all the blood had run out of his face. "Don't even joke." In this moment, all the worries in the world seemed to vanish, and the only Meredith was the only thing he could think of.

"Jan, you know I was joking. I don't want to die again. It was painful."

"Let's drive. I want to test out my new body a bit, and I was serious about needing new clothes. Can we stop off at home before going to the Vineyard? I don't want to be walking around naked. Jan looked down and paused.

"Anything for you, my love." Jan unlocked the doors to the car and opened the door for Meredith. On the way home, Jan noticed Meredith kept looking at her arms and turning her hands over. "Are you okay?"

"Yeah, I'm just admiring my new skin color. Do you think people will just think I spend a lot of time in the tanning salon?" Suddenly she gasped. "Do you think people will recognize me?"

Jan reached over and grabbed her hand. "I think your friends and those close to you will know who you are. You don't look different; you just have a slightly different tone to your skin."

With a sigh, she nodded and looked at the hand being held by Jan. "Thank you, I didn't think it would worry me as much as it does. I guess I got used to having slightly green skin."

"I understand. Just take it a day at a time, and we will for sure get you new clothes." Jan raised his hand and kissed the back of her hand. "I love you." Jan pulled into the driveway, and Meredith hopped out to change.

We need this to work. I will not lose anyone else close to me.

While Meredith was changing, Jan called Theo and Cee to let them know what had happened. He intentionally left out the fact he met their mother, or knowing Hades was at least partially responsible for this.

As he was talking, Panterra walked into the house with Sammy following along behind her.

When Sammy saw Jan, she took off and catapulted herself into Jan's arms, as only a boxer can.

Jan, I didn't think you were coming back. I heard Panterra tell them you went through the gates, and I couldn't talk to you. I was so scared. The dog's whole body was wagging.

"I see you missed me, but I'm alright. Trust me, okay?" Jan lowered Sammy to the floor, and she ran back to Panterra who was rummaging in the kitchen for food.

Jan shook his head while Sammy sat with her tail stub wagging so fast her entire back half was wiggling.

"Where are Cee and Theo?"

"Theo is helping take care of Hades, and Cee is at the vineyard with Brandy and Diana. Basil is also there because he heard there may be some fighting. I think he's been itching to fight again."

"Wait, why is Theo taking care of Hades?"

"Do you not remember? Hades was attacked by Set before—"

"What? Is he okay? No, I don't remember." Jan began to pace.

Pantera tossed a piece of meat to Sammy as they waited for Meredith to get ready.

The scene Jan walked into surprised him.

Theo was knelt beside Hades' grand bed. Lying there was a small, defeated figure. Hades had a bandage across his chest, and the once white dressings were turning a crimson hue.

Hades looked over as Jan and his entourage entered the room. He was about to speak, but when he saw Jan's look, he waited.

Jan walked to the foot of the bed, towering over the broken god. "I come from in the gate." Hades nodded knowing the secret was out.

Theo stood off to his right. "You mean inside the gate?"

Jan looked at his brother and nodded. Turning to Hades, all he asked was, "Why?"

Hades looked from face to face for any shelter but could not find any, even his dear Persephone would not protect him now.

"For the vision to work we needed a place for the souls to heal."

"You mean abandon," Jan cut in.

Hades sat up shaking his head. "No. No that was not the intent. But the Titans—their vision of the world was full of destruction. Humanity would not have survived. This world we live in now would never have been. Some think it's so terrible, but for those who have seen the world before this, it's a utopia." Hades winced at an onslaught of pain, taking a deep breath before continuing.

Jans gaze was unyielding.

"After the war was trending to our side much to the thanks of you, Jan, we had to create a place not only for the souls but also for the Titans. Some wanted to execute them all. But we found an alternative. The world above, a heaven of sorts, for souls to heal and calm before returning. And a prison for those who brought destruction and chaos. As we found, one could not be without the other. These worlds were unstable and took tremendous power to support." Hades paused.

"The souls, it's the souls." Theo began to remember. "The souls power the gates. You have used us to collect and drain souls." Theo stepped from the bed.

Jan stepped in before Hades could defend himself. "I've seen the other world. It's heaven for those souls. It's beautiful, and so is the caretaker."

Hades' head dropped.

"She chose to go. It was her, not me." Hades answered as Persephone stepped closer before grabbing his hand. Persephone spoke, "Your mother was a wonderful woman and a good mother. She knew the risks and the sacrifices being made in order to end the war. The death was mounting, and there were no other solutions to save the world."

"Why stop the coins from going over? Why not let them return?" Jan dropped a coin he had collected on the bed.

"We didn't know what would happen. If the souls returned, would there still be power to keep the furnace closed? Or even from collapsing? The world was small, and the population did not exist as it does today. Very few new souls were born at this time. We needed all the power we could get. If the furnace collapsed, so would the afterworld. It was a risk we could not take."

Jan was about to speak, but Hades lifted a hand. "She did not know, and even if she did, nothing would have changed." Hades sat up more, building up his confidence.

"The Titans may have turned on us, but they were still our people. And they did not deserve to be lost." Hades' tone was final.

"But why not now, why not allow those to return?" Jan said, relaxing his tone now understanding what was at stake.

"I don't know. The same fear lived within me. The world was safe. I have no other explanation." Hades again slumped back into bed, holding his side now completely dyed red with blood.

The group stood to leave, but Jan resisted the tide. "Why did we not know you were our father?"

Hades smiled. "Boy, you have always known. What is remembering a short life as a child compared to a millennium as an adult? I have always been here. You all just grew up and forgot." He looked from Jan to Theo.

Theo's face remained still. He had remembered, he always remembered.

Merideth grabbed Jans arm. "Jan, we must go. Set has the stones. I can feal the energy surging."

Jan looked at Merideth and saw the fear. "Theo." A second later his brother was gone.

Jan looked at Pantera. "Go fetch Cee and bring all you can." Suddenly, the room was empty save a broken god and his caretaker.

Theo had returned to the gate first and was watching what he could only describe as a gathering of forces. Before the gate stood a dozen or more warriors dressed from head to toe in battle gear. Their helmets were dark black with a red slash. Theo knew the more slashes on the helmet indicated a higher rank in the Titan army. The remaining armor was dyed a similar onyx black with red accents. On each of the solder's backs slung a spear which was accompanied by a short sword attached to their belts. The same armament the Romans utilized during the ancient human wars.

They were all Titans. How had so many evaded his brother during the war, or had Set recruited Gods to his side? A cracking behind him diverted his attention away from the gathering army. Walking up behind him in a hunched sneak was Panterra.

"Well, nice of you to finally show up." Theo looked over her shoulder. "Just you, I'm guessing? We're good, but... Ahh hell, we can take 'em." Theo laughed as Panterra settled down next to him.

"Look, I am good, but I don't know if I'm Titan Army good. Cee and Jan are bringing others. They contacted the Golems, and Dryads, so they should be here soon. I have as many Reapers as I could find enroute. But I still don't see our numbers being large, only around 20 or 30. I just hope they don't incre.." A massive vibration rippled across the battlefield, stopping Panterra's words.

They both looked back and saw the once silent gate bursting and crackling with energy. The rock arch rippled with vibrations almost like the stone had turned to liquid. The desert and rocky backdrop disappeared in the shimmering red light filling the void. Out stepped a figure, a woman.

Panterra gasped. "That's my mother!"

"Yeah, and she's not alone." Theo pointed at the others who followed.

Jan grabbed Theo's shoulder, causing him to jump. "Damn bro, not the time," Theo said.

"Yes, it is."

Theo looked back and saw dozens of figures in differing shapes and forms. "We need to close the gate before we're overrun."

"All right, all right. That's more my style." Theo's presence changed, and his blue eyes reflected off the armor his brother was wearing. "Game on."

Theo jumped from his hiding position and jogged toward their foe. He was met with the unsheathing of swords.

As he moved forward, swords appeared in his hands, and his clothes melted and shimmered like mercury, finally settling on silver battle armor covering his body from head to toe. His face was covered by a similar helmet to those of the Titan army, as well as his chest arms and legs. What differed was his armor reflected the light. He was a blazing sun moving across the void.

A step behind him was Panterra, Jan, and Cee. All with similar armor except Panterra. She wore black flowing robes which hid her movements, shadowing her abilities. She was but a shadow.

Theo admired her for a split second before turning back to his prey ahead of him.

The first sound of the clash came from Theo's sword finding its mark across a multi-marked dark helmet. The echo of steel on steel brought a familiar smile to the Cerberus brother.

Jan moved through the crowd avoiding slashes and thrusts from spears and swords alike. He was searching for Set. It didn't take him long to find the bastard.

Standing just off the side of the gate, Set stood holding a red stone against the arch. "Ahh, I see you have come."

He recognized the voice. Jan spun in time to deflect a well-aimed arrow.

"I have waited for this moment since the forest when we last met, Jannes Cerberus. I have prepared to kill you for a thousand years," the woman said rushing Jan, her bow discarded for a Roman Gladius. Before she could reach him, Panterra stepped in front of her, stopping the woman in her tracks.

"Mother."

Themis stopped, confused. Betrayed by her anger, her sword dropped slightly.

"You fight for them? Scum you have become! I have seen you and have heard you are standing in the way of our kind's freedom! You are nothing more than an obstacle now for me and your father." Her sword hand raised again.

"What are you saying mother? My father? My father is dead. You told me he was dead." The two faced off, standing feet from each other, weapons held high and ready to strike.

Jan had moved off as the battle raged. Two Golems had positioned themselves with a group of Dryads near the gates entrance and were attempting to cut down anything that came through. For the first few waves, the Golems had crushed the stragglers who appeared completely unprepared, but the titans changed tactics so more and more came through together.

The next group was 20 Reapers ready for battle. They came bursting out of the portal, red shimmering scythes in hand. The closest golem took the brunt of the attack and fell to the ground before turning to gravel. The other was not far behind, taking one Reaper down with him. The Dryads stepped over their fallen comrades, clashing with the Reapers.

The viscousness of the Dryads reappeared as their weapons sang in the air, many of them survivors of the great war fighting for their lives against the Reapers once again. Many had wished for this day for so long. It was a chance for revenge. The Reapers who came from the portal had been hardened in the furnace, but nothing prepared them for the hate they encountered.

The Reaper versus Dryad battle had grown as more and more came through the gate to replenish the fallen. Endless wave after wave of Reapers now joined by a few Titans pushed the Dryads back one after another until they fell, lifeless to the blooded soil.

One Dryad stumbled on a rock and lost his balance. His defense fell, and he found himself impaled on a Titan phalanx, never touching the ground. The remaining four continued to be pushed back. Another fell, killed by a Reaper's red scythe severing his head. The attackers paused, regrouping for their final push.

"Ahh." Bursting through the mix and joining the Dryads came a red-haired fury followed by Cee. The two smashed into the group flanking them. Half fell before they even knew they were there.

"The gates down! The gates do—" Came a yell from across the battlefield, the originator unknown and cut short.

21

Jan quickly re-targeted Set with the distraction of Panterra. He maneuvered himself quickly through the clashing soldiers, never taking his eyes off his target. A body fell before him, and he didn't look down to see if it was one of his or not. There would be time after the battle to count the dead. His chakrams came out, coming down on Set. The attack was ineffective.

Set easily deflected the blow. His hand was still firmly planted against the arch, powering the portal.

Jan was no match for Set, and he knew it, but the gate had to come down.

"Do you think you can stand against me? You scum, Hades' bastard son." Jan fell to the dirt, hearing but not hearing Set.

A dagger flew Jan's way, thirsty for blood, but it found itself harmlessly on the ground.

"My turn." Theo had deflected the dagger and jumped toward Jan in one motion. Sword coming down hard on Set's defenses, Set's face change from arrogant to fearful. Theo was a different fighter than Jan. Theo had fought much more than Jan, and Set knew to fear him. Theo was the Titan killer.

The attack caused Set to take a step back, pulling the gate from his outstretched arms. The shimmering red lights that had illuminated the sky disappeared, leaving long shadows with bursts of sparks from swords clashing in the dark.

*****

Panterra deflected blow after blow from the maddened woman she knew to be her mother. Panterra knew if she continued to defend, eventually she would lose.

Panterra sidestepped, running into a Reaper battling one of the remaining Dryads. She looked at him, recognizing his face from her time in the furnace. With one fluid motion, she left him dead in the mud. Panterra turned back to her mother just in time to deflect the blade she wielded from killing her into her upper leg. The pain raced through her body, and everything screamed. It all settled in her mind into a deep fury, which she unleashed.

Her leg did not slow her down as she pressed her attack on her mother. Slash after slash, she attacked, pressing and pushing. Then one, and another blow made it through.

Down went the Titan, falling to the ground, hands empty. Themis looked up, her expression changing from loathing, to fear, and finally understanding. "Panterra?"

Jan stumbled into Panterra while fighting a Titan soldier wielding a spear.

She side-stepped, allowing Jan's energy to take him on by. The soldier was unaware of the woman who moved in the shadows.

The Titan fell to the ground dead, landing next to Panterra's mother.

Jan's eyes followed the falling soldier as he landed on Themis. "We are meant to see this thing through." Jan held the woman at bay with his chakras.

She slowly stood, brushing herself off.

"We should. You sent me to hell," she said, eyes locked on Jan.

Jan sighed, lowering his weapons which disappeared in a woosh. "Yes, I did. Did I understand what was happening, or why? No, I was doing what I was told to do. Do you?"

She looked at him, confused. "You hated us, and you did this. The armies, the death, it was you. You hated us!" Her voice grew so loud, heads turned to look, and silence fell as all eyes found the two.

"Hate? You were the same as us. The Gods, the Titans—we are the same. Ask your precious Set, or Hades. What made us different was ideology. What to do with the souls." He trailed off, bringing his blades back up. "I don't want to fight. I don't want to kill Panterra's mother but trust me, I will if I have to if that's what it takes to restore order, to restore goodness and kindness."

"Do you think what you do is kindness? Is goodness?"

"Stop." Set ran over, stepping in between the two with one arm drooped at his side, useless and blood dripping from his fingers. A dagger clutched in his other.

Not far behind, blazing across the field, was Theo.

Jan's hand raised, stopping his bother.

Now all was silent. Jan looked at Set and how he protected the woman. "You did all of this for her?"

Set's eyes dropped.

"When you sent them all to the Furnace, I had no options. I was lost, the war was lost, my people were lost." He stopped, looking around.

"Why all the death? Weren't there other options?" Jan asked.

"Hades was, and probably still is, unwilling to change. He was unwilling to let the Titans go. I was only able to speak to my wife through Reapers. The scum they are." He hissed, looking at Panterra.

"Wife, father?" whispered Panterra, gasping with realization. She looked at her mother then to Set. "You are my father?"

Set stopped, whipping his gaze from the Reaper to the woman he stood protecting.

She grabbed his hand, letting the sword clatter to the ground. "It's true, she is your daughter. Do you not see it?"

He shook his head, tears welling in his eyes.

Jan looked around at the bloodied bodies and wondering souls. "It's time the Titans return. It's time we all come back together."

Themis looked at Jan. "No. The hate is so thick in our world if those gates open again, then we will wage an endless war. A war we have been training for, unfortunately." She looked at Set, her features softening and stroked his face with a bloodied hand. "We can still be together, but our time in this world has not come yet. Maybe one day, but not today."

Set grabbed her tight with his one arm. "Maybe you're right. Maybe you're right." He looked up at Panterra, with less hatred than before but said nothing.

"What are you saying?" Cee joined the party, red stone in hand.

"We should return to the furnace and make a life for ourselves there. Start working on putting aside our hate and maybe one day return a better people," Themis said, eyes locked on Set.

His shoulders sank lower, and blood still dripped from his limp hand.

"Then so be it. You have a life here if you wish. There's no need to return." Panterra looked between her mother and father.

Themis nodded. "Yes, there is. Set and I are the leaders, as is Hades to you. To change we must return. I will not leave my people. You put us there for a reason. Maybe we needed it to grow and instead we trained. This time it might be different. Maybe we can let go of the hate."

Jan nodded. "But if I open the gate, we will be overrun by your soldiers waiting on the other side."

"No, I can go. I can travel from our world to yours." Panterra grabbed her mother's hand. "I can stand before the gates on your side."

Themis nodded, looking at her hands before taking off a ring. "Here, take my ring, show them. They should listen."

Panterra held the ring, looking at it. It was a red stone with a raven in the middle.

Panterra disappeared.

"Wait, did she say should?" Theo's armor was gone, back in his regular clothes.

***

Jan took the stone from his hand and walked to the great stone gates. He took a deep breath; everyone knew the end could be soon. Jan lifted the ruby and pressed it to the stone. A great wave burst forth followed by a red glow that started in the center, rapidly spreading until the gate shimmered.

The brothers waited, anxiety growing as no one came.

Theo shifted his weight ever so slightly.

The Gate rippled, and a foot came forward followed by a hand. Theo relaxed, recognizing the ring held by the hand. Out walked Panterra, her black hair glowing.

"They agreed to wait for my mother and..." She paused, "and father."

Set nodded and moved toward the gate. He was followed by two remaining Reapers and a handful of soldiers. Each with loathing in their eyes as they passed the brothers.

Noticing the looks, Set stopped in front of Jan. "Maybe she's right. It might take time to live together. I would, in the future, like to know my daughter."

Jan nodded and stepped to the side.

Set looked at Panterra one more time before melting into the shimmering light, followed by his followers.

Last was Themis. "I hope you will come to visit. I'm sorry I never told you about your father. I was so angry, and I regret what I said earlier. You found a home with the Cerberus, and you are protecting your people. I just hope I can protect mine until it's time to reunite. Panterra, maybe, just maybe, you can help us rebuild and heal," she said, hugging her daughter before disappearing, leaving Panterra in tears.

The red glow vanished, leaving everyone in silence and darkness.

Hades stood looking out his window as he heard the door behind him open. He did not turn to see who it was as he knew it was over.

Jan walked over, putting a blood covered hand on his father's shoulder. "It's done."

Hades' head sank. "Are they dead?"

"No," Cee answered his question. "They returned in the hopes that one day they will be willing and able to return. It's no longer a prison." Cee had been brought up to speed on all the current events with the Gates and his lineage.

Hades turned to look at the brothers. Happy they were safe but with sadness and fear of what was still to come.

***

The water felt colder this time as Jan walked through the waterfall into the gate room. His mind was set, the promise made was going to be kept. He walked to the small desk and gathered all of the coins in the drawer. He added the coins from his pocket. The bag was filled with thousands of coins, and they clanked as he walked. He stepped to the gate holding a single coin in his hand.

"I will be here waiting for you." A sweet voice filled the chamber as he looked back to see his wife in all her beauty.

"I know." Jan lifted the bag and stepped through the shimmering gate.

Acknowledgements

We would like to thank both of our families for giving us the time to write this book. Five minutes here and there really add up.

We would also like to thank Melanie Marsh and Terry Journey for their editing skills. Without you two this would not be the book it is today.

Thank you, Covers by Robin, for the beautiful cover.

Thank you to the beta readers who were honest about what they liked and didn't like.

Finally, thank you to all of our readers who have been with us since Ancient Resurgence, and to all of the new readers. Without your support, we would not be able to write.

About Author

F.L. Journey is the pen name for two authors who have come together to write in a variety of genres they enjoy. Look for more short stories and novels in the future from them.

Follow us on Facebook, Goodreads, Bookbub, and Amazon. Look for announcements about, The Crimson Scholar, second in the Cerberus Brothers Series, which follows Cee and Turk.

By signing up for our newsletter, you will be sent exclusive content that spotlight all of the characters from the Cerberus Brothers Series.

Facebook: https://www.facebook.com/FLJourney

Other books by Author

Ancient Resurgence Series

Ancient Resurgence: Daniel's Story

Ancient Resurgence

Cerberus Brothers Series

The Cobalt Warrior

The Crimson Scholar

The Jade Commander (Coming 2024)

Matching Galaxies

Princess and the Pirate (Coming 2024)

Anthologies

Illusions – "Death Awaits" – July 2024

Little Witches – "Growing up Teen Witch" – October 2024